Cry of Vengeance

She felt a hand on her shoulder. A large man's firm grip steadied her and a very authoritative voice said, "He's gone, Missus. He's gone."

A knot big as Luther's fist refused to be swallowed in her throat. Gently she put his limp hand on his body below the arrows. Then, as if she was a little child, someone gripped her upper arms and lifted her to her feet. Tears burned her eyes like fire as she struggled up the loose incline to the wagon. Upon seeing an arrow embedded in the box, she broke it off with one hand and tried to squeeze the life out of it.

"Damn you red devils. I'll kill every one of you over this before I am through with you." Then she fell forward against her arms braced on the side of the box and cried hard.

DON'T MISS THESE
ALL-ACTION WESTERN SERIES
FROM THE BERKLEY PUBLISHING GROUP

THE GUNSMITH by J. R. Roberts

Clint Adams was a legend among lawmen, outlaws, and ladies. They called him . . . the Gunsmith.

LONGARM by Tabor Evans

The popular long-running series about Deputy U.S. Marshal Custis Long—his life, his loves, his fight for justice.

SLOCUM by Jake Logan

Today's longest-running action Western. John Slocum rides a deadly trail of hot blood and cold steel.

BUSHWHACKERS by B. J. Lanagan

An action-packed series by the creators of Longarm! The rousing adventures of the most brutal gang of cutthroats ever assembled—Quantrill's Raiders.

DIAMONDBACK by Guy Brewer

Dex Yancey is Diamondback, a Southern gentleman turned con man when his brother cheats him out of the family fortune. Ladies love him. Gamblers hate him. But nobody pulls one over on Dex . . .

WILDGUN by Jack Hanson

The blazing adventures of mountain man Will Barlow—from the creators of Longarm!

TEXAS TRACKER by Tom Calhoun

J.T. Law: the most relentless—and dangerous—manhunter in all Texas. Where sheriffs and posses fail, he's the best man to bring in the most vicious outlaws—for a price.

JAKE LOGAN

SLOCUM
AND THE
TEAMSTER LADY

JOVE BOOKS, NEW YORK

THE BERKLEY PUBLISHING GROUP
Published by the Penguin Group
Penguin Group (USA) Inc.
375 Hudson Street, New York, New York 10014, USA
Penguin Group (Canada), 90 Eglinton Avenue East, Suite 700, Toronto, Ontario M4P 2Y3, Canada
(a division of Pearson Penguin Canada Inc.)
Penguin Books Ltd., 80 Strand, London WC2R 0RL, England
Penguin Group Ireland, 25 St. Stephen's Green, Dublin 2, Ireland (a division of Penguin Books Ltd.)
Penguin Group (Australia), 250 Camberwell Road, Camberwell, Victoria 3124, Australia
(a division of Pearson Australia Group Pty. Ltd.)
Penguin Books India Pvt. Ltd., 11 Community Centre, Panchsheel Park, New Delhi—110 017, India
Penguin Group (NZ), 67 Apollo Drive, Rosedale, North Shore 0632, New Zealand
(a division of Pearson New Zealand Ltd.)
Penguin Books (South Africa) (Pty.) Ltd., 24 Sturdee Avenue, Rosebank, Johannesburg 2196,
South Africa

Penguin Books Ltd., Registered Offices: 80 Strand, London WC2R 0RL, England

This is a work of fiction. Names, characters, places, and incidents either are the product of the author's imagination or are used fictitiously, and any resemblance to actual persons, living or dead, business establishments, events, or locales is entirely coincidental.

SLOCUM AND THE TEAMSTER LADY

A Jove Book / published by arrangement with the author

PRINTING HISTORY
Jove edition / August 2010

Copyright © 2010 by Penguin Group (USA) Inc.
Cover illustration by Sergio Giovine.

All rights reserved.
No part of this book may be reproduced, scanned, or distributed in any printed or electronic form without permission. Please do not participate in or encourage piracy of copyrighted materials in violation of the author's rights. Purchase only authorized editions.
For information, address: The Berkley Publishing Group,
a division of Penguin Group (USA) Inc.,
375 Hudson Street, New York, New York 10014.

ISBN: 978-0-515-14829-9

JOVE®
Jove Books are published by The Berkley Publishing Group,
a division of Penguin Group (USA) Inc.
375 Hudson Street, New York, New York 10014.
JOVE® is a registered trademark of Penguin Group (USA) Inc.
The "J" design is a trademark of Penguin Group (USA) Inc.

PRINTED IN THE UNITED STATES OF AMERICA

10 9 8 7 6 5 4 3 2 1

If you purchased this book without a cover, you should be aware that this book is stolen property. It was reported as "unsold and destroyed" to the publisher, and neither the author nor the publisher has received any payment for this "stripped book."

Prologue

Under the fringed leather skirt, her cowboy boots churned through the heavy sand as she ran alongside of the wagon train toward the lead one. One of her teamsters was hurt up there. All at once, she lost her footing in the loose dirt and slid down the fill on the left side of her body. The fall hurt her hip, but her gun arm was still extended and ready. She swung the hat on the cord around her throat over her shoulder so it rested again atop her back. Down on her side, she looked underneath the belly of the close-by wagon for a possible shot at one of the Apache raiders. Nothing in sight.

Cussing under her breath, Willa Malloy regained her footing and scrambled up the loose, steep fill. Them damn Apaches anyway. On the bank again, she moved past the front truck of the third wagon. Jeff Ackers stood at his spring seat, firing his rifle at something out in the chaparral.

"You hit any damn thing with all those shots?" She talked more to his double team of mules, rather than him, so they didn't kick her passing so close to the near one's heels.

Upset, they stomped around, but were wedged in by the tall mesquite vegetation and the wagon in front of them.

"I got me one and a horse," he said. Then the rawboned teamster spit tobacco over the dashboard and wiped his mouth on the back of his hand.

She turned back to be on her way and smiled to herself. "Keep shooting, Ackers, at anything that ain't a haint."

"I will, little sister, I will."

At thirty, she didn't feel like little sister anymore, but most of the men that worked for her still called her that. At five-feet-four, she was no towering giant, but she made up the shortage of her height in pure grit. Fast getting out of breath, she came by Warren McCollough's rig.

"McCullie, you all right?" She stopped beside his seat looking up for his face to appear.

No answer. Scowling over his lack of showing, she scrambled up the wheel spokes and peered into the empty space ahead of the boxes of army freight and around the seat. He wasn't there.

Her boots on the ground again, she hurried to the first rig. McCullie poked his gray-bearded face over the side, looking upset at her. "It's Luther. He's got arrows in his chest."

Oh, dear Lord. She holstered her six-gun and climbed up in the rig to stare down at the man crumpled on the floor, sprawled half under the seat. Three feathered arrows stuck out of his chest, and the pained look on his fast-paling face told her lots that she didn't want to even imagine. Luther Gray didn't have long to live.

Searching around at the dense chaparral cover, there were no signs of the raiders that she could detect. That didn't mean they'd quit. That didn't mean they'd gone home to play house with some squaw. More likely they were either resting or out palavering in a group about what to do next.

"Some of you keep watch," she shouted, loud enough they could hear her at some distant Apache rancheria up in the Dragoon Mountains. "Three or four of you come up here and help get Luther out."

"Sister," Gray managed. "I plowed—a—bullet—in that damn—Whey."

"Take it easy." Already on her knees beside him, she felt sick at the sight of the arrows that stuck out of him.

"I believe—I got the sumbitch good."

"I sure hope you did." She clasped his rough calloused hand in hers. For a moment she fought back tears. Her real intention was to kiss him and smoother him with her body. Not because she had any or ever had any relationship like that with Luther before. Just her way to try and comfort him in his last hours on this earth. But the crop of arrows kept her from doing little more than kissing him.

Then she rose up on her knees, filled with a newfound hopelessness. "Hang on, Luther. Hang on, please."

Men were coming on the run through the tight confines of the thick brush and the narrow road. Soon, they gently lifted him out of the wagon bed, her scolding them the entire time to be careful with him. Then he was packed to an opening of the brush and laid upon a blanket on the ground.

"Take off his boots—carefully," she told them.

His knee-high boots were removed. Luther's deep cough, she knew, came from the blood flooding his lungs. And not a damn thing she could do to stop the bleeding or even a way to get him to a doctor. Even if one was available on the scene, he probably couldn't save the man.

His head propped up in her lap, she tried to smile down at him. "Why, Luther, you've won bigger battles than this."

"I fought at—some damn place during the war—hot as hell—hotter than Arizona ever even gets—I was shot there that day, too. But I promised my momma I'd come—"

His speech grew more slurred and his efforts to get air harder. "I'd come home to her and—I did. But, sister, you know what?"

"No, what, Luther?"

"She died before I got back there."

His thick hard fingers in her grasp and pressed to her lips, she wanted to scream. She wanted to escape the entire day and say it never happened. Oh, dear God, please help him. Please, please—

Then she felt a hand on her shoulder. A large man's firm grip steadied her and a very authoritative voice said, "He's gone, Miss. He's gone."

A knot big as Luther's fist refused to be swallowed in her throat. Gently she put his limp hand on his body below the arrows. Then, as if she was a little child, someone gripped her upper arms and lifted her to her feet. Tears burned her eyes like fire as she struggled up the loose incline to the wagon. Upon seeing an arrow embedded in the box, she broke it off with one hand and tried to squeeze the life out of it.

"Damn you red devils. I'll kill every one of you over this before I am through with you." Then she fell forward against her arms braced on the side of the box and cried hard.

1

General George Crook stood in his office with his back to the wall map of New Mexico, Arizona, and Sonora. He had a stiff posture, shoulders squared, that set him apart from ordinary men even out of uniform, which he seldom wore. This morning was no exception. His eyes hooded by his brows, he looked across the parade grounds at something. Few details escaped the man's eagle vision. The roof eave of the headquarters building kept him from looking at much of the mountain that rose to the south.

"Well, Slocum, you and Tom Horn didn't find out anything about the renegades in Sonora?"

"I guess they're having regular bowel movements," Slocum said, and stretched his dusty boots and spurs out in front of himself seated in the captain's chair.

"Good. I was worried they'd become constipated from eating rats and piñon nuts down there."

"There's only a handful of them left."

"How many?" Crook demanded.

"Less than fifty."

"Do you know what fifty Chiricahua bucks can do? Why, they can make a swath through Arizona like a sickle mower of dead ranchers, prospectors, women, and children—enough to make the San Pedro River run red with blood."

"But you've got every spring and water hole between here and the border guarded by buffalo soldiers."

"It ain't enough. Where are they at down there?"

"Sierra Madres."

"Hell, that's bigger than most Eastern states."

"I know. And I've seen most of those damn mountains over the past three months."

Crook used the flat of his hand to press down his hair from his forehead to the top of his scalp. "You don't want any more of this scout service?"

"A handful of Apache scouts is all right, but they can't take on Geronimo or Whey or any of those others in that bunch with that few fighters."

"Who really leads them?"

"You know you don't lead Apaches. They go with who they think has the strongest medicine."

"Who is that?"

"Geronimo."

"What about Whey?"

"He's the cruelest sumbitch down there. He'd kill you and then eat you to gain your strength."

Crook agreed with a stiff lip and a nod. "The slaughter last year of Lieutenant Kary and his patrol told me that he was insane."

The last cool breeze of the morning swept in the open double doors. Two troopers came inside, floured in trail dust. They quickly realized the general was there. Their spurs snapped sharply on their heels and they saluted him.

"At ease. Lieutenant Cosby will be back in a moment."

"Yes, sir," the sergeant said.

"What in the hell brings you two up here? You're with Hayes at Fort Huachuca, aren't you?"

"Yes, sir. I'm Sergeant Manning. This is Corporal Green. Apaches attacked a freight train bringing us supplies two days ago and killed one of the teamsters. A man named Luther Gray."

"They get anything?"

"No, sir, Mrs. Malloy is a tough gal. She even thinks Gray shot that chief called Whey."

"How sure?"

"It was the last thing he said to them. 'I think I got Whey good.' "

Crook shot a hard glance at Slocum. "That would be a real blessing."

Slocum agreed, then sat up in his chair. "Was this Luther Gray a Southerner?"

"Yeah, yeah," the corporal said. "I drank a few beers with him when he was down at the fort on other occasions."

"I'm certain he was one of my corporals in Virginia."

When Slocum finished, Manning went on. "All I know about this Whey is that he was supposed to be in Mexico. How in the hell did he get up here so quick?" Sergeant Manning searched their faces for the answer.

"Let nothing surprise you about the Apaches." Crook shook his head, then went back to pacing the floor. "They're like smoke and travel on the wind."

"That's why I'm here, sir. The telegraph wire is down between here and Huachuca and Captain Hayes wanted to know if we should take up his tracks across the border."

Crook shook his head. "Don't cross it. Those Mexicans don't want us on their side yet."

"Captain Hayes hoped we could have your permission to pursue him."

"No, not yet." Crook's scowl would have melted a gold bar close by him.

Manning accepted that answer with a nod. "Then we shall exchange our horses for fresh ones and immediately ride back down there. Captain's waiting on the word from you."

"Get some chow first and then do that." After saluting them, Crook looked at the ceiling for help. "The damn Signal Corps will look for days to find where one of those damned Apaches tied the wires together with buckskin. How in the hell did those indigenous bastards ever figure that one out?"

Slocum chuckled in his throat. "I have no idea, sir."

"Well, there is no talking you into staying in the service as a scout?"

"I'm not doing you any good, or myself, down there."

"Tired of Spanish women?" Crook shot an amused look back at him.

"I guess." Slocum started to rise out of his chair.

"I have a bigger need. You ride over for me and see what you can do for Captain Hayes about Whey. You know Whey. Maybe you can locate him if he was only wounded. If I am real lucky and he is dead, I'd be rid of half of the renegade leadership in Sonora, right?"

"Exactly. I'll go, but I may not stay. If it was a hoax, I'll be going on."

"Fine. I like a good understanding. Let's have some whiskey to seal our deal."

Slocum rose and went over to stand in front of the large polished desk. Some whiskey might go good at that moment. Nan Tan Lupan had outfoxed him again by not making him stay on longer to help him.

Crook retrieved a half-full bottle from his desk drawer and two glass tumblers, then set them on the polished surface. He popped out the cork and one-handed, splashed the golden brown liquor in each glass. Then he set down the bottle. "Here's to ending this war."

They clinked glasses and Slocum tossed down some of the smooth stuff. The sour mash cut the lacquer off his tongue and cleared his throat halfway to his balls. "Damn good stuff."

Crook nodded, looking again out the open doors at the empty parade ground. "Bring me back Whey's left ear, Slocum."

"I'll damn sure try, sir."

2

Slocum's mount was completely jaded when he, Manning, and Green rode their worn-out animals into Fort Huachuca stables area. Under the star-pricked sky, he dropped heavily to the ground. His horse blew dust with his nostrils close to the ground.

"Who in the hell's name rode these army-issue animals to their death?" a booming voice called in the night.

"Among others," Manning said, "General Crook's personal scout, Slocum."

"That you, Manning?" the big man asked.

"Yes, it is, Harris. And you get some men out here to rub these animals down and put them away in good shape."

"I can do that."

"I expect you can. Have a soldier show Slocum where the visitors' quarters are at."

"I know where they're at. I can find my way. Is Captain Hayes back from the border?"

"He rode in an hour ago," Harris said.

"Manning," Slocum said. "You better go break the news to him about the border business."

Manning agreed, handing his reins over to a green recruit. "He'll be mad as hell."

"It ain't our fault. Tell him I'll be by and talk to him about this Whey business in the morning." Bedroll slung over his shoulder, he started up the line of cottonwoods for the visitors' quarters. The long row of two-story officer homes faced the drive with their back doors to the dark, tall mountain rising above them. Nice place. Great climate. Aside from the large contingency of buffalo soldiers assigned there, it would have been a delightful place to serve— but the black units were considered by the officers in the ranks a non-promotion place to be.

But hell, they had too many officers that stayed in the service who once had been majors and colonels, and at that time they were lucky to have a captain's rank. During big wars like the last one, they needed them all—in these times, they cut the military spending so much, those still in were lucky to have shoes.

He though someone was sitting on the porch swing when he put his boots on the first step. But shadows hid whoever was there.

"Evening," he said, standing on the top step and looking back across the pearl star-lighted parade grounds.

"Evening," she said, and the swing began to creak.

"You're up awfully late."

"I could say the same about you, mister."

He used his thumb to tilt his hat back on his head. Still in too much darkness, he couldn't see her clearly. Short. Her bobbed hair color looked light brown, maybe blond, about collar length.

He sighed. "Just got in from Bowie."

"Go on inside. My room's the first one on the right. No one else's staying here."

"Guess I'd have plenty of choices then. I'm sorry, my name's Slocum."

"I've heard of you. Man used to work for me just died this week, told me many nice things about you."

"Luther Gray. I understood he was killed."

"Yeah."

"Sorry. Luther was a good man."

"You ain't needing work, are ya?"

He yawned and covered his mouth. "Not today."

"What about tomorrow?"

"I can't tell what it will bring. I never caught your name."

"Willa Malloy. I have a freighting business."

"I've heard about you."

"Aw, they probably said that I cuss too much for a woman."

He shook his head, and then dropped the bedroll off his shoulder to stand beside his leg. "No, that you are a legend at getting supplies to these forts."

"Yeah, and I may quit the damn business for good. My husband Mike was killed two years ago in a barroom fight in Tucson. I thought I needed this business to keep myself from going crazy. Now—it's making me that way."

"I hope we can talk more later." Slocum watched her pumping her legs back and forth so the swing would rock. He nodded and tipped his hat. "Till morning."

A red Mexican wolf up on Huachuca Mountain cut into the crickets' nightly serenade with a deep throaty howl. The sound echoed in the canyons twice. Then he went to wailing over again.

"I wish that horny bastard would shut up."

Ready to go inside the dim lighted hallway, he stopped and looked back at her. "He bothers you, come on to the second room. That'll be mine."

"I may actually do that."

"Suit yourself." He went on inside, lit a candle, and found

his room stuffy. He raised both windows and left the hall door open. The cooler night air came inside as he spread the bedroll on the floor. He hated bedbugs. When the bedroll was all rolled out, he toed off his boots, shed his vest, shirt, and britches. In his underwear, he blew out the light and climbed under the light blanket. In a few hours the temperature would bottom out in the canyon and he'd need a cover. His .44 wrapped in the holster near his head, he closed his eyes to the crickets, red wolf, and creaking of the house.

Uncertain how long he'd been asleep, he awoke to someone knocking. Rolled over on his belly and propped up, he was hardly able to see more than a short figure under a blanket standing in the open doorway.

"Yes?" he managed.

"I'm accepting your offer."

"Come on." He turned the cover back and then rolled on his side, anxious to get back to sleep.

She quickly obeyed and snuggled to his back with her arms hugging her breasts. He could feel her shaking. Was she that cold or that afraid?

"We need more blankets?" he asked.

"I'll spread mine over us." He felt her sit up and add the extra cover.

At last he decided, maybe if he held her, it would drive out the cold, and rolled over. When he did and pulled her up against his chest—he heard her suck in her breath.

"What's the matter?"

She wet her lips and took her time to answer him. "My husband's been dead for years—"

"I understood that."

"I've never been in bed with another man in my entire life besides him. I know—I know—people think I'm some army whore. But I guess when Luther Gray was killed two days ago—I went to pieces. I had no one to turn to. I'd been having nightmares about a big wolf jumping in a window and devouring me." She drew in her breath. "Ah, shit, you don't want to hear a crazy woman's going off at the mouth . . ."

He caught her chin and kissed her on the mouth. The longer they kissed, the more relaxed she became, until she threw her arms around his neck. Snuggled tightly to him, she at last buried her face beside his ear to catch her breath. "I'm going to owe you for tonight. Take me away. I'm yours."

"Let's go easy then."

"Oh, I don't—know, I'm so fidgety. I might back out."

"Start thinking about being on clouds and riding the wind on a flying carpet."

She laughed and raised her butt so he could push the blousy nightgown up past her waist.

"That's not going to work." She sat up and shed it over her head, then fluffed her Dutch-bob hair. He could see the outlines of her pointed breasts quake when she turned back to him. In his arms, she rode on his chest and began to pick at the buttons on his underwear.

"Hell, let's shed these drawers, too."

She raised up and helped him unbutton the one-piece down the front. With her pushing it off his shoulders, he felt her small, calloused hands on his bare skin and kissed her hard. Then together they struggled the underwear off him. At this point, she must have discovered his emerging manhood and she drew in her breath, trying to get her small hand around his stalk.

"Oh, my God. I didn't know men came in different sizes."

"It ain't how big they are. It's how you use it."

She nodded woodenly as he gently cupped her breast.

"I told you—I had no experience at this besides him."

"You don't need that either. Just let yourself go. You're still so uptight, either about us doing this, or that wolf out there, you'll never enjoy it unless I can get you to relax."

"I'm trying. I'm trying."

"You're still trying too hard."

His mouth on hers, him on his elbow, he slid his other hand over her muscle-hard belly. The slick abrasion of his tongue seeking entry in her mouth undid the last of her resistance. She widened the V between her legs for his entry, and cried out when he touched her most private spot. But she caught his hand and shoved it back in place before he could withdraw it.

Like a fiddle string, she began to mellow, and soon dropped her knees open for him to probe her deeper. Raising her butt off the bedroll, she increased her breathing, and despite the dim light in the room, he could see her eyes begin to glaze over. In those next few minutes, she turned from stone to pliable clay. Need gathered his body in a tight ache. He molded the curve of her breasts and heard her sharp intake of breath.

He rose and crossed over between her legs. Once over the top of her, he gently inserted his dick in her moist gates. She gave a sharp cry at his entry, then raising her hips, pulled him down on top of her in an open welcome to take her. Unconditionally committed, she arched her back to take all of him.

"I'm flying. I'm flying."

So they flew and flew. Despite the predawn's cool air, sweat greased their bellies and they fought to find the end. He kept pumping her twat harder and harder until he realized that deep in his scrotum the artillery was loading. He rode her with long hard strokes, while she rose up to meet each one with such force, he thrust the breath out of her, making her gasp with sounds of pleasure. All the way inside her with his back arched like a bow, he delivered his cum. He lay there panting and savoring each spasm.

"Oh, my—" she managed, and melted into a soft cushion underneath him. With the back of her hand resting lightly on her forehead, she shook her head. "I learned another thing for the first time—tonight."

"What's that?" he asked, sitting up on his knees between her legs.

"Every man doesn't do it the same way either." Her hand rested on his thigh with bold familiarity.

"Did I pass?"

"Pass? What're you talking about?"

"Did you like it?"

She struggled up on her elbows. "Enough. I'd rest you all day for the night work."

He shook his head and grinned. "Can you sleep now or do you need another round?"

She peered at him in the dim light with a look of disbelief. "You serious?"

"About doing it again, yes."

She blew out her breath. "My land's sakes. Let me sleep a few hours and then can we do it again?"

"Whatever. It's your call." He smiled to himself as she turned on her side against him.

He pulled up the covers and then curled around her. Thirty minutes later, with all thoughts of their sleep forgotten, their raw closeness and a hunger for each other brought up a need that struck them again.

By dawn, he was yawning his jaws open and dressing while seated on his butt. She'd gone next door to put on her clothes. Strapping on his holster last, he went to her room, where she had gone to dress.

"Do you think Luther really shot Whey?" He stood in the open doorway.

"He said he did before he died." Busy brushing her hair furiously, she paused to clean out some of the loose hair from the bristles. "He wasn't a braggart nor did he ever lie to me."

"I knew the man. No word on if they learned anything about Whey's death?"

"No, they've vanished like they always do."

"Hayes's man, Sergeant Manning, thinks they beat it back to Mexico."

"Why not? The U.S. Army can't chase them down there. Poor dumb Mexicans can't fight them, and they won't let our men do it."

Slocum nodded. "What are your plans for today?"

"Mine?" She blinked in shock at him for asking.

"Sorry, if it's private."

"No, no, I wasn't expecting you to ask me that."

"Why not?"

"I thought most men got what they wanted out of an affair and ran off somewhere to brag about it. You have a wife?"

"No."

"You should." Then she put her hands over her mouth, snickering about the idea. Her amusement soon turned into red-faced embarrassment.

He walked over, hugged her to his waist, and looked down into her blue eyes. "I had fun last night. I'm not opposed to doing it again."

She looked at the sky and drew in her breath. The thunder of boot heels on the porch moved them apart.

A young red-faced private burst in the front door and announced, "Captain Hayes wants to talk to you at once, sir."

Slocum nodded to her with a private wink. "See you later, ma'am."

3

Slocum and the private headed for the mess hall. Red-faced, Captain Benjamin Hayes came bursting out of the bachelor quarters. "Slocum, hold up!" Half dressed, he finished putting on his blue and gold jacket before he extended his hand to shake with Slocum.

"Let's go eat in the mess hall. What in the hell's Crook's problem up there?"

"It ain't Crook. It's politics between Washington and Mexico City. Them folks down there ain't forgot what we did to them last time we were in their country."

"My God, man, that was clear back in the thirties."

"Them Mexicans got a good memory of that ass whipping."

"Hell, we're only chasing a handful of Apaches."

"Crook's hands are tied. Does your intelligence think that Luther shot Whey?"

"My intelligence is right now probably down in the town, drunk on their backsides in some sleazy brothel, trying to catch a new case of clap."

"At least they aren't out where the buzzards can pick out their eyes. Other words, you don't know shit about Whey or his condition or if he was shot at all?"

"Exactly. I only know what I've heard. Mrs. Malloy spoke to me about the matter when she first arrived in the fort. Anything else was gossip on the wind. We couldn't be so damn lucky as to have one of them lead bastards dead." Hayes opened the mess hall door for Slocum to go ahead.

Then he turned and said to his aide, "Private Cozzy, have us two horses saddled. Make it three. We may all three ride down to where Santa Cruz flows in out of Mexico and speak to Meyer Arnold. He knows more about what goes on down in Mexico than anyone."

"My saddle is down there at the stables," Slocum said after him. Cozzy nodded and hurried off to obey his orders.

"Good boy," Hayes said. "I understand that back home he got the local mayor's daughter knocked up and he was not who the mayor had in mind as his son-in-law-to-be. So he gave him a choice, either join the army or go to prison on some trumped-up charges."

When they were seated in the officers' mess, a KP served them coffee and took their order for eggs.

"Fried, over easy," Hayes said, and turned to Slocum.

"Scrambled like the rest of me."

Hayes was in a chair across the table doctoring his coffee with sugar and canned milk. "You've been in Mexico recently?"

"Yes. Tom Horn and I were in the Madres for six weeks with a handful of scouts."

"Have any luck locating them?"

Slocum shrugged and lifted his steaming coffee, letting it soften the beard stubble around his mouth. "They're down there all right. I told Crook they were there and not constipated."

"Did he laugh?"

"I can't recall exactly, except he mentioned he was glad they weren't constipated from them eating rats and piñon nuts."

"So why are you here?"

"Hell, I wanted to resign. There is nothing we can do with only a handful of scouts to hem them in. You know Crook. He talked me into coming down here and finding out all I could about this Whey incident."

Hayes nodded sharply and then blew on his half-milk, half-coffee. "If something hadn't gone wrong in that raid, those bucks would have finished off Mrs. Molloy's bunch in short order and taken what the hell they wanted and then pissed on the rest."

"I think you're right. Something went bad wrong. They wiped out Lieutenant Kary and his men like they were toy soldiers. What, a year ago?"

"About that long. Her outfit would have been a damn sight easier to massacre. I've ordered a patrol to meet her outfit halfway from Tucson each time she comes down from now on. Nice lady." Hayes shook his head, then looked around to be certain they were alone before he spoke again. "I'd damn sure like to have her in my bed."

Slocum casually nodded. Right. She wasn't half bad in *his* either.

Their food plates, delivered to him and the captain, were heaped with eggs, biscuits mounded high with flour gravy, crisp bacon, and fried German potatoes.

"I get all this eaten, I'll be ready to shovel out the stables," Slocum said.

"Better eat well while you can." Hayes used his fork to make the point. "In Mexico, I bet you ate enough beans to fart the canyons full of gas."

"I've ate my share."

Between his forks full of food, Hayes managed to say, "I'd hoped we could have pursued them."

"Anything to get off your ass?"

"Exactly. Southern Arizona is not the tourist capital of the world, and never will be more than a few adobe jacals, some sidewinders, and a few chaparral birds darting around. Hell, there ain't half enough water in this country to do anything. We damn sure didn't get much buying this land from Mexico."

"We've got a snow-proof route for the railroad to the West Coast."

"And hell, we can't even get it built across through here."

They finished their meal and when they went outside, Private Cozzy had their horses ready in front of the mess hall.

Hayes stretched his arms over his head in the early morning sunlight to the crackle of a thousand birds using the green oasis the army had set up for their border operation. "It's a real paradise here."

"Not a bad place," Slocum said, then thanking Cozzy with a nod for the reins as he handed them over to him. The tall, leggy bay acted alert enough when he prepared to mount him. Once in his saddle, he reined him up. His choice of horseflesh and the supply officer's actual pick were two different things. He wanted a mountain horse, short coupled, handy as a cat on the steep trails, and able to survive on what he could find in this arid land. The army wanted a cavalry horse that could answer the bugle and charge across a level field. There were damn few such fields they'd fight over in Arizona or northern Mexico that would meet those criteria.

"Your horse all right?" Hayes asked.

"Yeah, he's part Thoroughbred."

Hayes laughed, drawing his horse up beside him. "Which end? The front or the back?"

"I'm not certain about that yet. I'll let you know later."

"Cozzy, wasn't that horse you secured for Slocum one of the best in the stables?"

"Yes, sir."

"See what we have to put up with?"

"You go to Mexico on these New York street cop ponies and you'll be afoot in three days. The horse I rode over here on from Bowie I bet never makes another trip."

"Oh, so you see the problem. Will you tell Crook I need better horses?"

"I'll tell him, but I don't know the good it will do. Your own quartermaster bought these animals, I'd bet."

"And he buys stolen Mexican beef from Ike Clanton's man as well."

"You want to sell beef to the army or Indian agents, you have to go through Ike."

"Part of the damn system. We're fighting a fucking war with our hands tied behind our back."

"And Eastern newspapers say the army has overemphasized the entire Apache problem."

"Yeah, have 'em tell that to Randolph Taylor, who lives outside of Patagonia. They kidnapped his wife and teenage daughter two years ago and no one's seen them since. Or the Cripps family over by the Dragoons. All of them tortured and then murdered. It goes on and on."

"All overexaggerated."

"I ever get one of their reporters out here, I'd overexaggerate him."

They arrived at the river crossing in late morning. Hayes led the fording. Swift water ran almost to Slocum's mount's knees in the deepest part. They were soon across, and the horses shook as hard as they could to throw off the water clinging to them.

The series of adobe buildings marked the trading post and cantina. A tall man with a snowy mustache, wearing a gold-braid-decorated, tan civilian waistcoat, stood under the palm frond shade of the porch.

"Good morning, *mis amigos*."

Hayes nodded. "We are looking for lunch."

"Come inside. I have some fresh barbecued *cabrito* for your noon meal."

"Meyer, this is Slocum. He's a scout attached to General Crook's office at Bowie."

"Nice to meet you," Arnold said. "What can I do for you?"

"There's word that Whey was shot in an attack on a wagon train taking supplies to Huachuca."

"I have heard that, too."

"What do you think? Whey survived or not?"

Arnold clapped his hands, and four women came into the room. "Ladies, fix my friends here, some *cabrito* and frijoles and tortillas," Arnold said to the women, who looked to be waiting for the word. They scurried off, and soon great-smelling food appeared.

"I also heard that Reynaldo Garcia was making a guns-for-gold swap with the Apaches," Arnold said.

"Who's he?" Captain Hayes asked.

"A local *generale*. You know about him, Slocum?"

"Yes. The central Mexican government hires some private concessionaires who supply them soldiers-of-fortune armies. Garcia does this out of Arriba. What makes you think he's taking them arms?"

"Oh, Señor, I listen to the winds and also gossip. It will tell you things before they happen."

"That's how you learn in this country," Slocum said.

Hayes nodded in agreement and began filling his plate with the barbecued goat meat and the frijoles set out on the table.

"Getting back to Whey," Slocum said, topping his plate full of food with some very fresh flour tortillas.

"Oh, I hear some small things. They say they rushed Whey to a doctor."

"A doctor?"

"Yes, a white doctor."

"Where at?"

"The word was it was a white man's gun shot him and a white doctor could cure him."

Slocum frowned before he took another bite. "Who would that be?"

"I am not certain, but they couldn't take him far, could they?"

"He's a tough old bird. Depends how badly he was shot up, of course."

"Would you pay me to hire some boys to go check on all the medical doctors around here? They can find out and see if we can trace him from there?"

Between mouthfuls of food, Hayes asked, "How much would it cost?"

"Ah, say twenty American dollars."

Hayes looked at Slocum. "I can afford that?"

"You're footing the bill," Slocum said. "But I'm sure Crook would agree to that much money being spent on such a cause."

"Then tomorrow," Arnold said, "I shall send out ten boys to learn if Whey came by for treatment."

"Good. It would make a starting place," Hayes said, and wiped his mouth on a cloth napkin, then motioned his hand at the man. "Great food."

"Thank you."

Slocum's thoughts went back to Reynaldo Garcia. The man was a backstabber, a liar and cheat. The very mention of the big man's name made Arnold uneasy. Garcia would do anything to make a peso, including forcing his own grandmother to work in a whorehouse.

After the fine meal, Slocum and the other two rode back to Ft. Huachuca to wait for Arnold's report on Whey's medical treatment, if anyone knew a thing about it. It was way after suppertime when they arrived back at the fort on their jaded horses. Slocum decided that if they had to chase Apaches in Mexico on those mounts, the Apaches would escape them riding jackrabbits.

"This horse situation is terrible," Slocum said to Hayes. "Those horses we brought for Bowie were just as bad. One good ride and they caved in."

"They're all we have."

"Well, I can tell you right now, you try to ride into the Madres on horses like them, you'll be foot soldiers in two days."

"It's serious—the horse deal. But for now, let the mess hall feed us," Hayes offered as they walked up the fort road toward the main buildings and officer row in the twilight.

"We'll eat. Right, Private?" Slocum asked Cozzy.

"Yes, sir."

The food dished out to them at that late hour bore no comparison to the rich-tasting meal that Arnold served them earlier, but Slocum decided it would fill some space in his empty guts. After the meal, he thanked the two and went off to the visitor quarters. At the base of the steps, he halted and looked at the swing in the final shadows with the sun beyond the horizon in the west. Empty. He'd kind of hoped that she might still be there.

Oh, well. He started up the steps and looked in the dimlit doorway. No light shone in her room. They'd never mentioned that morning about getting together again. Perhaps she'd left. He drew a deep breath and went inside the softly lit hallway.

"Learn anything today?"

He smiled, grateful that she was standing there just inside the open doorway to her room. "We're trying to find out if Whey was treated by any doctor in Mexico and what was his condition."

"No news?"

"No, but we have several folks looking for answers."

"I wondered if you'd even get back tonight."

He bent over and hugged her. "I was coming."

She swept the hair from her face and pursed her mouth for him to kiss her. Then he took her up in his arms and carried her down the hall to his room. "What occupied your day?"

"I hired a new driver to take Luther's place. He's young, but stout and should work all right."

"When're you going back to Tucson?"

"Tomorrow. I'll be back in a week."

He set her down. "Nothing turns up about Whey, I may go on."

"Where to?"

"I'm not certain. I'm tired of not getting anything done about these renegades." He dropped to his knees and then gently laid her on his bedroll. "Mexico won't let us chase them across the border. Their army is afraid of them. I told Crook if things didn't get to moving, count me out."

He bent over and kissed her as he undid his vest buttons. Before he could shed it, she pulled him down on top of her and kissed him hard. When she came up for air, she was gasping. "Damn you. What did you wake up inside of me?"

He squirmed a little to be comfortable on top of her and the long gown she wore. Braced up over her face, he smiled down at her. "So I cut it loose, huh?"

"Yes. I've been getting along fine for two years—not even thinking about it, and I woke up this morning—well, you were gone and I was so heated up—I tried to use my finger. But that's a damn poor excuse for having a certain man in me."

"You must not have been very far away from it for me to wake it up."

"You sure opened my cave door." She laughed and wiggled suggestively under him.

He kissed her again. His hand lifted her gown, his palm sliding over her silky legs. In anticipation, she spread her legs apart and he gently began to probe her with his middle finger. In minutes, her butt was off the bedroll. She twisted and thrust to match his actions. Her heavy breathing grew loud as he teased her ear with his tongue.

She tore at the buttons on his shirt until he stopped fingering her and began to undress, gripped by an urgency to be naked and inside of her. Quickly, she shed the gown over her head and on her knees helped him to take off his pants. Shirt gone. Boots off. His frantic fingers undid his underwear. When it was open at last, his erection flew out. She caught it and her lips closed on the tip.

He felt ready to scream. Her tongue rasped the ring of the head and made him want to soar off like a screaming Chinese rocket. The next few minutes jumbled his mind as she took all of him in her mouth. Then, when he thought he would scream, she moved under him and pulled him down on top of her, and they scrambled to connect.

His great lance entered her lubricated walls and she gave a small cry, "Yes, yes, yes . . ."

Her back in a U-shape to accept all of him, he pressed harder and deeper with each stroke. Their friction burned the coarse pubic hair between them. His butt was driving her hard and the need grew inside of him to explode. His breath raged through his raw throat like a forge being pumped more air. Then something gripped his balls in a vise. He felt the lava rise in his tubes, and then the molten rock exploded out the skintight head of his dick—they both collapsed.

"Slocum, Slocum." She rolled out and climbed on top of his chest. "Where did you ever come from?"

She buried her face in his chest to kiss him and then laid

her head on top of his breastbone. "My, my, that was not sex, that was something else. Tell me about your life."

He pulled her up higher and kissed her willing mouth. "I came from Georgia. My family had a farm before then. The war killed my mother. Broke her heart. My father couldn't live under their jurisdiction. He died. I shot a federal judge, which caused him to die. And I left Georgia."

"You have no wife, no roots?"

"None, except you here tonight."

"What a waste. You've spoiled me. I never ever escaped to another world doing this before. God bless his soul, my husband loved me and I figured he did the best he knew how. But he never awoke the wicked *bruja* in me like you have. First, well, he wasn't made as big as you, and second— oh, when I first saw yours I thought that huge thing—well, I first figured it would rip me open, but it didn't.

"Whewie, I mean—" She swept the hair back from her face with one hand. "It is just crazy is all I can say."

He raised up and kissed her. "Don't worry, it's still there."

She rolled her gaze to the ceiling and let out a slow exhale. "Guess we aren't getting much sleep tonight either."

He hugged her hard and kissed her. "That's up to you."

4

The next morning, no word yet from Arnold was what Private Cozzy told him. Hayes was in a staff meeting. So Slocum trailed along after Willa's fringed hem while she checked on her wagons, mules, and men. He met the individual teamsters, shook their hands, and listened as she told them how McCullie would be in charge, and the army was going to escort them back and forth at least halfway to ensure they made it.

"Won't be the same without you, little sister," McCullie said.

She held up her hands to cut off their protests. "You men know more about freighting than I'll ever know. This deal over Luther has struck me so hard, I'm taking a little time off to try and find myself again."

They surrendered and nodded that they understood.

"Now you'll be leaving tomorrow at daylight. God be with you."

"You, too, little sister," the voices said in a chorus.

She turned, wetting her lips, and Slocum could see she

was close to crying. Everyone seated around the wagon camp looked upset when she left them, headed away in a fast walk. Slocum held his hand up to hold them off. "Give her some time. She'll be all right."

"Thanks for looking after her," McCullie said and the others added their approval.

When he finally caught up with her, he said, "Slow down. The worst is over."

She turned her tear-stained face up at him, still not missing a beat of her fast walk. "No, it's not over. It won't ever be over. My life—"

He caught her by the arm and swung her around into him.

Her arms encompassed his waist and she cried on his vest. "No, no, nothing ever goes right in my life."

He looked up at the towering Huachuca Mountain. He'd find them some solitary place up there. "Let's get some horses, foodstuff, and go hide out somewhere in the high country."

She looked up and blinked her wet eyes at him. "Where?"

"Oh, somewhere on those mountains where no one can find us."

"Never find us—oh, yes—let's go."

"What about the rest of your freighting business?"

"I have a good accountant and man in Tucson, Phillip Tate, he can fill the orders and the army is going to guard it. McCullie can run the wagon train part. I just want to get away."

"We'll line up some horses, a couple of pack mules and supplies, and head out in the morning,"

"What about your scouting deal?"

"I already told Crook I was leaving the service if something didn't break loose on this impasse over the border crossing. It hasn't and doesn't look like it will."

"Then we better go into Sierra Vista and find us some saddle stock."

"Let's go."

By noon, they had two stout, bulldog mountain ponies to ride. The kind that could handily scale steep mountains, live on dry grass, and carry a big man all day and not peter out. Both geldings stood perhaps twelve hands, a dusty red roan and a blood bay with a white blaze on his face. Four or five years old. No shin splints, freshly shod, and ready for the long ride if needed. These horses had a swinging walk that most horses would have to trot to match.

After his experience with military remounts, Slocum was pleased with their luck in finding such prime riding stock. He was on his haunches dickering over two pack mules. Beside him, with a week's whiskers, was Lyle Hartman, the livery man, who was spitting tobacco out of the side of his mouth, and the more they talked about the mule trade the faster he spat.

"I've got to have a hundred apiece for them mules. Hell, Slocum, the quartermaster will pay more than that for them when Crook gets ready to jump that border."

"I doubt that ever happens. Besides, he'd issue you a warrant for the cost and you might not get to cash it for a year."

"Aw, it would be good—someday."

"I like the two darker mules, but the shorter one is too old. He's getting gray around the mouth."

"They sold him to me for a nine-year-old."

Slocum shifted his weight to his other foot. "Nineteen, maybe."

"That gray is broke to ride."

"You could see him a mile away." Slocum shook his head.

"Hell, you going spying?" Hartman looked around for Willa.

"She's getting the packsaddles picked out and pads."

"Whew. Wish I was going off with her instead of you," he said under his breath, then turned his head away and spat loudly. "That is one fine package of blasting powder."

Slocum nodded in agreement. "How old is the gray?"

"Dead broke and five."

"So he's seven."

Hartman shook his head in pained disgust at Slocum's comment and wiped his bristled mouth on the back of his hand. "Business is a little slow right now. I'll sell you both the bay you want and the gray for a hundred-fifty."

"Bring them on."

Hartman struggled to his feet and laughed. "You're harder to trade with than any Scotsman I ever met."

"I don't have all day to argue is all, or I'd got you down some more."

Hartman was brushing off the seat of his pants and grinned big. "I would't waste this much time away from her sweet ass."

Slocum clapped the man on the shoulder and laughed. "She's been widowed a while."

"Hmm." Hartman snuffed at the notion. "Why, I ain't even in her class."

"A good shearing and some clean clothes, you might impress the lady sometime."

"You reckon?" Hartman squeezed his chin as if considering the matter.

Slocum nodded and they went in the pen to catch his mules.

By noontime, they were back at the fort and loaded their things on the pack animals. Slocum rode over to Hayes's headquarters and left word he was leaving. And for them to wire Crook good luck and if he learned anything he'd send him word.

Riding beside her in a jog trot under the warming sun, he wanted to circle the range and come in from the east. There was a good spring over there where they could camp for the night. Then they could make Cox's meadows the next day by noon.

The next day they were pushing their mountain ponies single file up through the live oak and juniper. The steep narrow trail was well worn, but at this point, when they rode by a spot where the brush was out of the way, they could look a hundred miles off into Mexico or that far north up the San Pedro basin.

"It's pretty up here," she said from her position in the lead.

Riding drag, he nodded. "Good isolated country."

"We all alone up here?"

"Probably, unless some old prospector comes through."

"Good." She turned back and pushed the bay on up the steep pathway.

By the time the sun reached one o'clock, he had a canvas shade hung at the edge of the grassy meadow that ran off between the slopes timbered in pine.

"I love this place," she said, returning with an armload of sticks.

"One of the islands in the sky. There's several around, but this is the one I like the best."

She dropped the wood on her pile and ran over to hug him. He bent down and kissed her. The contact broke all restraint and in minutes they were stripping off clothes and unable to take their eyes off each other's action. Soon, white flesh began to sparkle in the sunlight, and he swept her up and carried her to the bedroll.

There would be lots of distraction in this camping business with her. Lots.

Later that evening, they were seated around the glow of

the campfire and listening to the crickets, and a red wolf off in the distance, when he heard the sound of a horse's hooves crunching gravel on the trail.

"Oh," she said, and jumped up holding the blanket shut to hid her nakedness. "I better get dressed. That's someone coming."

"It damn sure is. Now who in the hell could that be?" He went to buttoning his shirt and tucking it in his waistband. The mules were honking at the intruders as Slocum buckled on his gun belt.

Who was out there? He glanced over at the firelight's reflection off her short shapely legs being concealed by the buckskin skirt she was drawing over them. Tying it at the waist she looked more satisfied with her bare butt finally covered.

There was more than one rider. Slocum tossed some more branches on the fire for lighting purposes. The cool night air carried the sounds of their hard-breathing horses pulling the last grade. Stepping back, she came under his left arm.

"I wonder—"

"We'll know in a few minutes." He felt her shiver under his hand. "Not to worry. They may be lost."

5

"Ah, you are Señor Slocum. I am so glad we found you. I am Fernando Morales. We met one time, Señor. I work for Señor Salazar at his hacienda in Sonora. May I dismount?" The great barb horse that he rode was spinning the roller in the spade bit with his tongue and he stomped in place. Three other riders remained behind him on equally excited animals.

"Sure. Good to see you again, Morales." Slocum started to step forward to shake his hand. "He's a good man," he said to Willa. "What brings you to my camp, Morales?"

"A terrible thing has happened, Señor. The Apaches have kidnapped the patron's lovely daughter Estria."

He shook hands with the man in the tan waist jacket with fancy piping. Morales pushed his hat off on his shoulder and then he spoke to Willa, "I am sorry to bother you too, ma'am. But this lovely girl is so important to my patron and his wife, who is so wrought up over the matter."

"I would be too," she said.

"What can I do for you?" Slocum asked.

"My patron believes that you are the only man that can get her back from them. He would pay a large ransom or do anything just so she is alive and safe once again."

"What Apache has her?"

"The one they called Whey?"

"He eats white men for breakfast. How could I do anything with him?"

Morales shook his head. "These are bad times, Señor, and there is not much anyone can do. But Señor Salazar will pay you a thousand dollars to try to get his lovely daughter back and give you all the support you need."

Slocum shook his head in defeat. "It isn't the money. It's the fact this man is crazy. No one can deal with him."

"He came to the white doctor in San Miguel to be treated for some gunshot wounds. Estria was taking her great-aunt there to see the doctor and got caught."

"Whey must have lived through his wounds?" He turned and looked at Willa.

She nodded she'd heard them.

"Please. Just do what you can to get the girl back. We know of no one else who might succeed."

Slocum folded his arms over his chest, then looked down at his dusty boot toes in the fire's orange light. "I hate to take your man's money on such a senseless mission."

"The señor is not a poor man. He can afford what he is offering you and more."

"But there is no way I can ride into Whey's camp and negotiate the return of some girl. Geronimo, I might, but this man Whey is rabid."

"If you would try for one month, I would bring you the money."

"Let me think it over. That is a powerful amount of money. Let me think it over tonight."

"Fine," Morales said.

"Señor Morales, have you and your men eaten supper?" Willa asked.

"We eat some beef jerky, but we might fix us some *pinole* at your fire if that is all right?"

"Tell them to come and do that," she said. "I have plenty of coffee and hot water too."

"*Gracias, señora*. That is very kind of you."

Slocum hugged her shoulder. "That's good hospitality. I had not heard of that kind of generosity often in the folks I travel with."

"You need to change company maybe?" She winked at him.

Slocum watched them take some of the hot water and pour it in their cups and stir it with a stick. A gruel of ground corn and brown sugar was what such men lived on traveling.

"We will move down the valley when we are through," Morales said. "We don't want to disturb your camp. At dawn, you can tell me your wishes."

Slocum nodded in agreement. But he couldn't think of a reason to go on another endless search. Hell, he'd quit Nan Tan Lupan for the same reason and he owed Crook more than he did Salazar. The men thanked her politely when they finished and rode off.

Slocum and Willa sat by the dying fire, alone at last.

"Can I go with you?"

"Where?"

"To try and find her."

Slocum shook his head. "I'm not going looking for a needle in a haystack that I can never find."

She hugged his hand in her lap. "Yes, you are."

"How do you know that?"

"'Cause of how God made you."

"What's he got to do with me?"

"I am not certain. But there are rumors that you are one of those men who took on armies to save individuals."

He laughed. "Wrong guy."

"No." She rose on her knees and cupped his face in her hands. "You are the one who brought a young boy home who had been kidnapped by Indians up by Preskitt."

"Those were Yavapai."

"There are several other stories. If I had been her grieving father with that much money, I would have come and asked you to get my daughter back." She bent over and kissed him hard on the mouth.

He hugged her to his chest. "All I wanted to do was stay up here and make love to you until our supplies ran out."

"We can do that too. I'll go along."

"Oh, yeah, then I can fetch you back from them."

She straightened his face with both her hands to look him in the eye. "I am going along. Now let's go to bed and we can finish this conversation later."

He swept her up in his arms and headed for their bedroll.

"I can walk," she said.

"I know, but I like to carry you. Makes me feel *macho*."

"Hell, if it does that carry me." She laughed and then quickly kissed him.

Alone in their end of the valley, there wasn't much sleep time. They sampled each other's bodies and after each encounter, fell asleep and woke in a new fury for more.

He discovered her nipples would get hard as pebbles when he teased them. She found her hand could awaken his shaft with little effort. She told him, snuggled in his arms, that her power to do that amazed her. And with their bodies connected, they both became carried away in a frantic way to reach new heights of pleasure.

In the predawn, he sat dressed and cross-legged as she

hurried about making a meal for the men. Not a word had been said since the night before about his decision.

Bent over frying strips of salt pork, she looked up and nodded at him. They were coming. The clink of their spur rowels and their boot soles on the rocks told him they would soon be there.

Somewhere, a dove cooed and the smell of her cooking smoky pork was in his nose.

They all tipped their hats to her and she carried the coffeepot around to fill their cups. Morales came last and sat beside Slocum. He held out his tin cup for her to fill it.

"*Gracias, Señora.*"

"Most folks call me Willa. Those that don't call me that call me Little Sister. I like Willa better."

"Ah, *sí*. You will be Willa from now on."

"Good."

Her fried pork and pancakes finally filled the hollow bellies around her fire. She swept the hair back from her face. One of the men called Raul asked her what she called them.

"Pan-cakes."

"Ah, *sí*. Pam-cakes."

"That's close enough." She laughed and began gathering her things to scrape and wash. But they wouldn't let her and made her sit down.

Morales and Slocum walked off to be by themselves.

"That is a good woman you have," Morales said.

"Willa is a fine lady. Apaches killed one of her men last week. She wanted to be away from everything and I brought her here."

"I am so sorry I interrupted you and her."

"No problem."

"Will you accept my patron's generous offer?"

Slocum looked at the ground. "I can't promise him nothing. I will go look for her. Did Whey head for the Madres after he left this doctor?"

Morales looked like a man terribly relieved at his answer. "Yes, yes, he rode in that direction. We were afraid if we got too close, he might kill her."

"You did the right thing. He might have. He has a very short fuse."

"How will you handle it?"

"I'll go up there and stay in one of those villages where the Apaches come to trade and try to set up a swap. When I need the ransom, I'll need it in a hurry."

"Estevan can go with you, help you, and then deliver the message to the patron."

"He can't go with me dressed like he's dressed today. I want him in sandals, white clothing, and a pony, not riding a great horse."

"Oh, I see. He would draw too much suspicion up there dressed like he is today."

"Right. They would think we were with the *federales* or something. He can be our guide."

"Ah, *sí.* I would never have thought about that. It might work."

"We're going to try hard. But I can't promise you a thing."

"Oh, I understand. So does the patron. But he needed to try something, anything, everything. "

When the hacienda men rode off at last after packing the mules and doing everything they could do for Willa, she turned to Slocum. "What did you tell him?"

"That we would go up there, live in a village where the Apaches come to trade, and try to barter with them. Estevan, the youngest, is going to be our guide up there. But I wanted him dressed for the role as a *peon*, not like a *pistolero* for a hacienda."

"Oh, I can see that."

"Good."

"What is her name again?"

"Estria Salazar."

She hugged his arm. "This will be a real adventure. I'm so excited."

"It will be a dangerous one. Keep that pistol of yours close by."

"What made you change your mind?"

Slocum shook his head. "Who knows, Willa? Who knows?"

"I think God knows. Where do we camp next?"

"Tonight at some rancheria between here and there."

"Let's ride, big man."

Let's ride sounded good, but he still carried a lot of dread about the future riding out of their camp.

6

"Are those soldiers?" she asked in a guarded voice.

"No, they're mercenaries," he said as they sat their horses concealed in a grove of mesquite trees and watched the company of men towing a light cannon with a six-horse hitch, crossing the open desert beyond them and headed north.

"How can you tell?"

"That color of tan material is not Mexican army issue."

"What're they doing with a cannon out here?"

"Crowd control. Heavens, I don't know. But I'd bet that Generale Garcia is involved with it."

"I've heard of him."

"Last word I heard was that he was trading guns for gold with the Apaches."

"But he's—"

"Right. He's supposed to be supplying troops to the central government and that ain't shooting square. But in Mexico you go where your bread is buttered."

"Has he made any such trades?"

"No, I think we'd heard of them crossing the border.

Crook has a good eye out for all arms shipments from anywhere in Arizona or New Mexico entering Mexico. But I ain't saying they couldn't cross at Juarez where the General has less control and come in the Madres by pack train from the east."

"Where are we going tonight?"

"The Valencias' hacienda. You'll like Lou and his wife Reba. We can rest there a day and Estevan will catch up with us."

"How far are we from the mountains?"

"Oh, two days, maybe more after today."

"There is lots of nothing out here. How does that young man and his children where we stayed last night under that ramada ever exist out here?"

"He wants to be a rancher and has a registered brand as well as some cows. He catches mustangs and breaks them to sell for his food money."

"But his wife, the poor thing, died in childbirth and she must have been young."

"Maybe he'll find him a new wife."

"How could he feed any more kids?"

"I never ask those people how they do that."

"But he sure did not turn you down giving him that sack of frijoles."

Slocum smiled. "On my salary this month I can help him."

"We haven't made it to the last day of this month yet either." She laughed. "My husband, God rest his soul, was such a worrier. He made one out of me. What do you worry about?"

"Oh, what those wild men are doing to Estria for their cruel entertainment and how we can ever get her from their clutches."

"That's something to fret over, huh?"

"Yes."

She booted her pony in beside him. "And you said that you weren't the man that rescued such captives."

"I have failed before too."

"So what. You have more success than anyone." She rode in closer and playfully swatted him on the arm.

"This one may crash and burn too."

"Let's lope a ways. It's not too hot today."

"Fine."

With him hurrying the mules, they cut a dusty trail eastward. By late afternoon, they were in the Valencias' citrus orchards and vineyards headed for the main headquarters.

She rose and twisted in the saddle to look over the greenery. "There are no rivers or lakes around here. How do they farm out here like this?"

"Artesian wells."

"I know all about them. They come out of the ground under pressure when drilled. Isn't that something?"

"It's made him and his family very rich."

"I can imagine."

"They make some great wines. You'll get to taste some of it tonight."

"I can't wait."

Lou Valencia came from the house dressed in a silk shirt and coat with a fancy scarf around his neck. "Ah, *mi amigo* Slocum and his lady—" For her he made a deep bow. "So good to have you here, *mis amigos.*"

Slocum tossed the roan's reins to one of the stable boys who had come on the run to take their horses and mules. Then he helped her off her bay.

"We are glad to be here. This is Señora Willa Malloy. My good friend Lou Valencia."

"Ah, what brings you to my *ranchero*?"

"Looking for a young woman kidnapped by the Apaches."

"Oh, how serious. It is her daughter?" Valencia indicated Willa.

"No, Willa is a widow. This girl belongs to the Salazar family."

His face paled. "Oh, not Estria?"

"Yes. The crazy one, Whey, took her."

"That is so bad. It will make my wife cry to hear about that."

"I'm sorry."

"No. No. I am so glad to see you and you too, my lady. Company always livens up the hacienda. So few people find us out here." He spoke to Willa, "Let Juanita see you inside, I must show Slocum my new stallions."

"I'll be fine." Then Willa spoke in Spanish to the woman sent to assist her. They both were soon laughing going to the house.

"She must be some woman?" Valencia said after her.

"She lost her husband two years ago. A week back, Apaches made a raid on her wagon train and killed one of her lead teamsters. She is on a forget-it-all with me."

"I see. You will love this great horse I bought six months ago. He came from North Africa. He is a breath of the desert wind."

Soon the main stable man led the high-headed, dish-faced stallion out in the bright sunlight. The stallion chortled deep in his throat, as if dreaming that perhaps there was a mare in heat outside there for him to service. His pale coat was cast in a red finish on a white base. Mane waving in the wind, he looked very expensive.

"I'll have his first colts on the ground in October."

"He looks very sharp."

"At seven furlongs, nothing has ever been close to his tail either."

"I guess they give horses like that away on race day down at Vera Cruz."

Valencia laughed. "Ten thousand dollars—gold."

"Put him in the barn, the eagles may want him."

They both laughed.

Slocum saw several of his other studs, but the red roan was his choice and they moved off to the main house. Reba, his wife, came rushing to hug him and brag on his companion.

"She is so nice."

"I guess she doesn't think I have abandoned her?"

"No, she is getting bathed and fitted for supper."

"Thanks, she needs some spoiling. She lost her husband and her *segundo* in the past two years or so."

They went on to the living room for wine, crackers and cheese. Willa soon joined them in a borrowed green silk dress and with a fresh look on her suntanned face. The material made a crisp sound as she crossed the tile floor with a wide grin. "Ah, such hospitality. How will I ever repay you?"

"By being our guest again," Lou said and laughed. "There is no need to concern yourselves. Reba and I spend most of our time here on the place. We have so much going on year-round. Once or twice a year, we get away to Mexico City or Vera Cruz. Otherwise, we are nailed to the job and can't go visit all our friends."

"I hardly keep a place in Tucson," said Willa. "I am on the road with my wagons all the time. So I am grateful Slocum invited me to go along with him. This ranch is so lovely."

"Tomorrow I will give you a tour," Lou promised. "Unless this man has to hurry on."

"We can take another day," Slocum said. The horses could use the fine care, feed and rest before they pushed on hard for the mountains. Maybe Estevan would also show up.

"Wonderful," Willa said with a pleased smile. "I will get to see your hacienda."

They drank the ranch's own smooth wine and a young man came with a guitar and played ballads. His tenor voice carried in the high-ceiling room and they applauded each song. Willa came over and stood close to Slocum.

"I could never have imagined our evening here would turn out like this. Isn't he good?"

He nodded and studied the tiny freckles on her neck and the tops of her exposed cleavage. "It is very unusual in the midst of the desert."

"They have no children?" she asked behind her hand.

"One son who is in Spain studying at a university."

"My, they must miss him."

Slocum agreed.

Then the music turned up a beat. "I could polka to that," he said.

She bowed and held up her left hand for him to take it. They went whirling around the tile floor like they'd danced together all their life. Spinning and laughing, they were alone in the great room and flying free as if no one existed until the song ended and the Valencias applauded.

"Thanks," Willa said to him. "I haven't done that since I was seventeen in west Texas."

"It has been a while for me too."

"Supper is ready," Reba said, and invited them in the dining hall. "Someday I want you to polka me around like that." She laughed and hugged Slocum's arm, steering him into the other great room.

Lou sat at the high-back chair and oversaw the serving dishes being brought around by the servants.

The roasted lamb, beef, and fowl came with potatoes, white and sweet, gravy, fresh-cooked green beans, traditional frijoles, fresh-sliced fruit, and hot rolls with butter. Willa looked shocked at all the spread of food and the fussing over them by the servants.

"I finally know how royalty really lives," she said under her breath to Slocum.

He smiled and agreed.

"This is wonderful," Willa said to their host and hostess. "I must say that you two can certainly entertain visitors."

"As I said," Lou began. "It is the thing we do best and enjoy doing so much."

After supper, they retired to their room. She stood before Slocum in the flickering candlelight and had him undo the corset laces. With the back of the gown open, he slid his hands around in front and cupped her firm breasts encased in the corset. Nibbling on her neck, he felt her shiver. "It's been a fun night so far."

She sighed and turned her face up for more of his attention. Already her nipples were growing hard, and she slipped the stiff undergarment down and tossed it in a chair.

Using him for support, she stepped out of the dress and fluffed it some before putting it over the same seat. "Best dress I ever wore in my entire damn life."

"I imagine so."

"Why, I bet it cost a fortune and there's a whole closet full in different sizes for their company to wear."

He pulled her to him and smothered her mouth with his. She had the heat turned on, and soon they both were busy undressing him. His boots were off. The gun belt put up, the vest off, then the shirt, and at last she tore open his pants to get at his rising shaft.

Her small fingers closed around his rigidity and she sucked in her breath. "I still could not believe it fit the first time. But it did—"

In one great sweep, he lifted her up and then dropped her in the deep feather bed. On his knees, he climbed across the springy surface to find her. Her tight breasts pointed at the ceiling when he came between her soft thighs. His erection throbbed in time with each long wet stroke in and out of her. Underneath him, she squirmed to get herself in a better place and they went on.

He plunged deeper and deeper inside her contracting walls. Their breath became short and the urgency grew greater and wilder. Her bare heels beat on his back as they went on and on. At last he exploded deep inside her with her clinging to him.

They fell asleep in each other's arms. Before dawn he rose, thinking he should wake her, and then he decided to let her sleep a while longer.

He found the kitchen crew busy gossiping in the room that was filled with the smell of food cooking and being prepared.

They brought him coffee. He had fond memories of this bunch from previous stops at the hacienda. One time the red-haired, sassy one they called Rojo had taken him in the pantry and given him a real wild blow job to show that she wasn't afraid of him or his big dick. There was the tall girl from Sonora who challenged him to screw her on the table one morning. So far he had not seen her this time, but he never forgot doing it to her standing on the floor and getting cheered on by the rest of them.

"Ah, you have your own pretty woman this time with you," Rosita, the head of the kitchen, said aloud.

"Yes, is there anything I can do for you?" Slocum asked her, taking a cup of coffee from one of the younger ones.

"No." She shook her head, laughed, and with a head toss indicated the other women in the room. "Some of them are the ones that need you, not me."

They all laughed. A few younger ones blushed and turned back to their work. They served him scrambled eggs, goat cheese, and spicy sausage rolled in a large flour tortilla with green chili sauce. Fresh, hot, and delicious, washed down with more coffee. He let them do their work and went outside to look around. Birds were singing in the citrus trees in the yard, and he could hear the stallions complaining down at the stables. Somewhere beyond the compound walls, milk cows were being gathered to drive in for the morning milking.

Things were coming awake on the Valencia hacienda as

the purple dawn crested the horizon in the east. The coolest time of day swept his face with soft breaths of the wind. Would be nice to have such a complete empire as Lou had there. But he was too sugar-footed to ever stay that long in one place.

And besides, the rancher had people to feed and clothe— his work force was numerous—still, this ranch was like heaven. A total escape from the steep poverty found in so many rural villages, the young daughters who were sold into sex slavery, the graft and corruption of the law that lived off bribery and under-the-table income. Mexico had some good sides, but underneath it was a much different way of life than the States.

Willa took Lou's tour of his *ranchero*, and by siesta time she was back at the great *casa*. Sweeping the wide-brimmed sombrero off her head, she fluffed up her hair while coming in the bedroom door.

"My, what a great operation," she said.

"It is nice," Slocum said with his back to the headboard of the bed.

"He has wonderful things growing all over. I ate a melon that one of the field hands brought me that tasted like honey, it was so sweet."

She crawled across the bed and framed his face in her hands to kiss him. Their mouths meshed and he pulled her higher up. In seconds his hand was feeling her left breast and she trembled at his touch—

"Oh, my God. I'm going to miss you someday . . ."

7

Before the sun even cracked the eastern sky, Slocum and Willa left. He wanted to be close to the Madres in another day. Pack mules in tow, they pushed hard all day to reach a small village called San Carlos. They watered their weary mounts at the village well and he fed them corn in their feed bags.

She found a vendor to fix them some frijoles burritos. While they were eating the spicy food, the village priest, Father Mullens, came by and offered them the use of his empty stables and corral for the night.

Slocum thanked him and they moved their stock into the shelter. There was enough hay in one crib for them to sleep on. So they unloaded their animals and let them roll in the dust.

"No one's going to have to rock me to sleep tonight," she said, undoing the bedroll in the starlight and rolling it out.

"We must have fallen from favor to have to sleep in here tonight," Slocum teased.

"Ha, I would sleep anywhere with you." Then she poked him in the muscle-hard gut with her flat hand.

"That's fine."

"You expecting anyone to disturb us?" Busy undressing, she paused for his answer.

"No, why?"

"Then I'll get plumb naked and see how tired you really are."

They both laughed.

Riders out of the night charged into the village. The commotion they caused awoke him. The invaders sounded half-drunk and were shouting demands in the dark. Six-gun in his fist, Slocum rose on his knees and tried to see who these hell-raisers were at the well.

Shots shattered the night. "Send your women out here, *hombres*. No! We will fuck them so hard, they won't need any more breeding for a month."

More shots cut through the night, followed with brave talk about the studs that they were. Then a woman screamed and Slocum could hear the intruders' laughter. Obviously, she was being dragged to the well in the center of the small square.

Slocum set his revolver down on the bedroll and began dressing. These bastards needed to be shot. He shook his head when she grasped his forearm and tried to stop him.

"There must be three or four men out there. What can you do?"

"Stop them," he said through his teeth and went on pulling up his pants.

Another woman's shrill protest cut the night as she too was dragged kicking and screaming into the center of all their activity and the raiders' raucous laughter rang out. More shots.

"I found more pussy, *amigos*. Here is another."

Willa was not to be left behind. She made him wait on

her while she dressed, and then with her gun in hand she came after him. He took a route around behind the buildings facing the square. Ahead of them in the dark shadows, he could hear a man grunting away—obviously, from the sound, he was screwing on the ground some uncomfortable groaning woman.

Slocum turned to Willa and put his finger to his lips. Then, taking soft steps, he was soon behind the man and struck him over the head with his gun butt. The outlaw went facedown on top of the woman and she screamed.

"Hush," he said, not wishing to draw any of the others into the alley. With the man separated from her, Slocum ripped off the man's bandanna and tied his hands securely behind his back. The young woman scrambled to get her skirt down and cover her nakedness.

"I need a gag for him," he said to Willa.

Without hesitation, she quickly reached down, tore a strip of cloth off the victim's skirt hem, and handed it to him.

The donor soon stood against the wall, biting her nails and nodding her approval.

The man lay on his side in the dirt with his pants down to his knees and his erection dissolved. Bound and gagged, he wasn't going anywhere—for certain not to rape any more women that night.

Slocum heard another intruder coming and forcing a protesting female ahead. The three plastered themselves to the wall to let him go by and then Slocum saw his chance. He stepped out in the narrow walkway and clubbed the man twice over the head with his Colt. Willa yanked aside the hysterical girl he'd nabbed and made her be quiet.

Girl number one jerked the pistol out of the man's holster while Slocum tied him with the lead rope for his horse that the raider carried around his waist. With him bound and gagged, Slocum left him facedown in the dirt.

Willa came back from the end of the alley, where she'd

been spying on the ones in the square. "Let us women handle them out there. We can conceal these guns against our skirts until we are close enough not to miss."

"How many are left?" Slocum was concerned about their welfare.

"Four. Right now, they are all busy raping women. We better hurry."

"Shoot carefully," he said, and they hurried to the square. He went left and stopped to club a man deeply involved in screwing a woman on a porch.

Shots sounded and two rapists bit the dirt. A fourth one ran off, trying to pull up his pants and screaming, "Don't shoot! Don't shoot!"

"I'll get him," Slocum said and tore after him. The man cornered a building and knowing he was unarmed, Slocum never paused. He spotted him climbing a rail fence and heading for a patch of corn. In seconds, he'd be gone into the shadowy stalks.

Three women joined him and each carried a six-gun in their hand.

"Is he in there?" one woman asked, motioning toward the moonlit stalks.

Slocum nodded.

The older woman directed one of the sisters to go right, the other to go left. She said to Slocum. "You get on the far side, we'll send him right to you."

Forced to keep down his amusement, he frowned at more shots he heard fired back in the square.

She shook her head. "They're only executing those bastards."

Executing? He shrugged and set out to go around the patch for the delivery of the last one.

"Throw your hands up, you horny bastard, or we'll blow your balls off when we find you," she shouted. "Get him, girls!"

Slocum was soon around to the far side of the corn patch waiting, wondering if his own life might be cut off in their wild cross fire. The women's anger rode on a thin edge and they were determined to clean up the entire gang.

The hatless outlaw burst out of the stalks headed for the fence, but his silhouette was barely against the sky when the red flames of their pistols blasted him off the top rail. They must have shot him a half dozen times. The bullets sounded like they were striking a watermelon. His body fell hard astraddle the rail fence, but that never pained him. He was already dead.

A woman under each of his arms, they dragged their trophy back to the village square. The others were laid out in a row of bodies and someone held a candle lamp as the padre prayed one at a time with each of them.

Willa came on the run to join him. "You all right?"

"I'm fine. I guess we've got them all?"

"Yes, they say these bandits have been doing this often for over a year. Get drunk, come over here, and rape all the women and even little girls."

Slocum nodded. "I knew there weren't any angels in the lot of them. Well, they have them stopped. And now they know how to stop any more from running over you."

"Señor, Señor," the woman in charge called out to him. She carried the hem of her skirt in one hand and ran over. "We want to have a celebration. This time we cleared San Carlos of the bad ones. You must join us. You showed us the way to do it and it is over. No more crazy fuckers coming here and raping our women."

"You did well today. But will they fight like tigers next time?" he asked her.

"I am uncertain, but tonight we must celebrate. Please join us."

He agreed and hugged Willa's shoulder. "I guess we can sleep anytime."

"Sure, anytime."

The red wine flowed. Women cooked. Slocum appreciated the way that Mexican women were able to serve a meal at a moment's notice. They butchered goats, pigs, and chickens and had them ready to eat faster than anyone could ever imagine.

Seated cross-legged on a braided rug with Willa, with the guitar music ringing in the night, Slocum licked his greasy fingers for the mesquite-smoked flavor from the *cabrito*.

Ah, viva Mexico.

With Slocum, hungover, seated on his saddle and hauling the pack mules, and with Willa not looking much better than he felt bringing up the rear, they left San Carlos. The first time that he felt the needles in his ears, he knew it was the mountains causing the pain. Later, climbing into the foothills and gaining altitude by noontime, he had a worse headache.

"We're going to take a siesta early today," he said to her. "I'm taking Mountain Fever."

"What's that like?"

"Bad headache, dizzy. It can get worse, but we can rest and I'll get over it."

"I won't argue. It's been all I can do to keep my eyelids open all day."

"Whew. There is a spring with some willows a little further. The willow bark will stop my headache. It's like someone drove a spike in my head."

"That beer was bad last night." She shook her head and the wide sombrero swung from side to side.

"It wasn't beer, only *pulque*. That's fermented corn."

"It was still bad."

He didn't bother to tell her how wild she'd been, a little drunk and worked up. She was an eager lover to start, but intoxicated, she became a fierce mink in heat. Keeping his newfound secret to himself, he pushed his horse up the steeper gravel trail. Cumulous clouds were building. Those up toward the peaks, he could see, were growing into columns. There would be thunder showers somewhere in the Madres. Every day in the monsoon season, rain fell in some parts of the Mother Mountains. Maybe only a passing shower or a gulley washer that would send dry washes to high flood stage in minutes.

By noon, they camped at a spring that came out at the base of a tall sheer buff and boiled over into a large rock basin. The spring's water was cool and refreshing. He tossed his hat aside, doused his sunbaked face in the clear liquid, and came up tossing his long hair.

"What do we need to do about the willows?" she asked, seated on the ground, pinching off green grass.

"Oh, make some boiling water. I'll scrape off some bark and we can make willow tea."

"I'm ready."

He winked at her. "Altitude. At times it really gets to me. I never know when it'll hit me."

"I'll get a kettle of water boiling."

He rose, went to the weeping willow tree, and began cutting off slivers with his jackknife. With a fist full of the bark shavings, he went to where her fire licked the black bottom of the coffeepot. Seated cross-legged again, he cut the bark up into smaller pieces. She brought him a couple of tin cups and a third one to put the tea in they didn't use.

"What woman taught you about the willow tea?"

"I'm not sure, but it's brought me around when I was lots worse than I am today."

"Maybe she had some charms you didn't see and it wasn't willow tea at all that cured you."

"No, I've done it without her too." He smiled at her chiding him. "But she may have been a *bruja*."

She smiled and rose on her knees. "The water is boiling. What do I do next?"

"Put a teaspoon of chopped bark in each cup and pour in the hot water. Then it needs to steep."

"That's easy enough. What is in it that helps you?"

"Some chemical that's in the bark, I reckon. Indian women keep it on hand in large supplies."

"I just wondered. How far are we away from those villages we are going to?"

"Maybe an eight-hour ride. But my head's going to be better before we go much further or higher."

"What else would clear your head?" A smug know-it-all smile written on her lips, she handed him the steaming cup. "Is it ready?"

He winked and nodded. "I'll check it."

When the tea cooled enough to drink, he found it had a *wang*. Sipping on it, he felt satisfied that relief would soon stop the sharp needles in his temples. Their camping spot was off the main road, the two dried up ruts that wound their way up into the Mother Mountains.

He used the downtime to bathe. She did the same, as well as shaved him. Then she washed their clothes and hung them on bushes to dry. They took siestas, and the mountain fever had began to release its grip on him enough for them to have a smooth round of lovemaking. When it was over, she sat up and grinned big at him. "Helped your headache?"

"Damn near gone."

They laughed.

Later in the night, he awoke to the sound of horses and mules. Quickly, he reached over and smothered her mouth. "We've got company and I ain't certain it's the good kind. Better get dressed."

"Who is it?" she hissed, already pulling on her skirt.

"A big pack train."

She nodded and went on dressing.

The fact that this outfit was moving at all so late after sundown made him doubly suspicious. Unusual for a packer to chance a night movement, especially in the mountain terrain they'd find ahead. They must be moving guns or other contraband to the Apaches.

The spring couldn't water that many animals. Slocum's wishful thinking said maybe they'd move on without trying, but taking no chances, he grabbed up the bedroll and told her under his breath to go saddle their horses. Rolling it up, he listened to all the confusion out on the road and braying jackasses, which was covering their escape. Soon mounted, they rode up the side canyon leading the pack mules. Feeling apprehensive, Slocum kept looking over his shoulder into the dark night for any sign of pursuit.

When they topped the next rise, he stopped under the weak starlight and they both listened. He could hear the distant cursing and mules protesting in the darkness as they went up the mountain.

"Have they gone on?" she whispered.

"I hope so. I could have slept a few hours longer."

"They must be in a big hurry to get wherever they're headed."

He wished he knew why. "Yes, traveling into those mountains at night is damn dangerous."

"What are we going to do?"

"Take a new trail in there." A less-used one, he hoped.

He damn sure wanted no war with the bandits. He was there to rescue or ransom a girl, not fight for some revolution or be in a power war for command of a region. Leave all that to the hired guns and soldiers of fortune,

The trail he chose proved to be a dim one under the stars that followed high-pitched hogbacks with a narrow path on their crests and thousands of feet on either side to fall if your mount missed a step. Her shadow was silhouetted ahead of the two mules he drove across the backbone.

"How much more is there of this?" she asked. "This scares me more and more by the minute."

"Keep your faith. It isn't far."

"You said that last time I asked. Sweet Jesus, this is like walking a rope. I saw a man do that over the street in Tombstone. My heart was in my throat the whole time for him not to fall. Here it's choking off my breathing."

"Try to settle down. There is no turning around. We're committed."

"I want to be on my hands and knees."

"Willa, close your eyes and relax."

"My heart is pumping so hard that it's thumping inside my chest. I close my eyes for very long, I won't ever open them again."

"Yes, you will. Yes you will. Be brave, we'll make it."

Hours later, on sea legs, they dismounted in a grove of pines, grateful to have gravelly ground under their soles. Her arms wrapped around him, and her whole body trembled as she clung to him.

"Did you ever use that horrible trail we came across back there before?" she managed to ask him.

"No, and I won't ever again unless it's to save our lives." He buried her sobbing face against his lower chest. The trembling in her shoulders and body continued. Anxious to relieve her of the trauma gripping her soul, he cupped her face and smothered her with kisses. Lips pressed together in wanton need, they finally slumped to the ground and soon they were lost in passion's arms. Her dress wadded up to her waist with her legs and crotch exposed, he tore open his pants and started his aching dick inside her.

When he opened her gates, she cried out and they fell into an abyss deeper than the hogbacks had straddled. Later, exhausted, they undressed and crawled in the bedroll. Nothing woke them until dawn.

8

The next morning, they sat cross-legged on the ground when the sun tried to come over the Madres. Blowing on his coffee, he wondered where that pack train in the night before was headed.

"I guess we're lucky we weren't discovered back there, huh?" she asked.

"Chances are we were lucky. They weren't moving at night because they wanted it known, I'm certain."

"I expected any moment to be discovered."

"They were so involved in keeping the train going, they missed us."

"What were they hauling, do you think?"

"Maybe guns for the Apaches. You know there's gold up in the Madres. Indians used to burn paper money when they found it on raids. They hated gold diggers. Now they know the difference. They've figured out what stolen money, and even what raw gold, will buy them. And there's enough greedy white men in this world that will exchange with them."

"Don't they know any better?" She made a pained face at him. "All the people that get killed—"

"They know better." He nodded with a grim set to his mouth. "I call it greed."

After a short meal of some crackers and dry cheese, they saddled up.

Slocum leaned over the saddle to speak to her. "There's no easy way into those mountains. The way that we're going eagles might hate."

"I'm with you. How's your head?"

"No worse."

"I'll make you some more willow tea later today."

"That'll be fine."

He wasn't about to tell her he had needles again in both ears piercing his brain. If he had the time, he'd have rested at the those springs another day before venturing higher and let his body adjust to the altitude. But he worried there might be some *pistoleros* with the pack outfit running as guards front and back. With a boost, he put her in the saddle and they headed out.

By noon, they were climbing into the Mother Mountains on a narrow trail notched out of the stone face. The clack of their shod saddle horses' shoes striking rocks rang like bells.

"Don't look down. It'll make you dizzy."

She threw her chin up. "No-no worry. I'm looking for a buzzard to float by close enough to pet."

He chuckled and looked ahead at the winding ribbon that angled skyward. If only his head'd quit pounding. His hand on the horn, he had to stay conscious until they reached the top, and by his estimate that was three hours ahead, with few places except some turn-backs wide enough to rest. Damn, he might have made the wrong judgment choosing this narrow staircase and him not feeling any better than he did.

With her bringing up the rear, they clacked up the mountain trail. His head-bobbing horse made his way handily. With lightning pain blasting through his brain, he tried to simply keep himself in the saddle and going on. All he had to do was ride. His left foot scuffing the rock wall and thousands of feet to a sure death under the right stirrup didn't mend his headache or stop the dizzy spells that swept through him in waves.

He was sweat-soaked more from the tension than the heat, but the wind striking him made a cooling sweep of his face that he felt grateful for. This day proved worse than the hogback one for him. He rode the horse more by grit than anything else. The sharp knives in his ears pierced painfully into his gray matter. Made him wonder why his blood wasn't squirting out of both of them.

Hours went by and deep in his lost mind, he knew she must be under a similar pressure. Then, he felt in his dull awareness his horse gathering himself under him in cat hops that about shook him out of his saddle. Like a giant hole cut in the sky, he emerged onto a flat land of pines.

Thank you, Lord . . .

He could hear her calling to him, but she was far away. How could that be? She held him in her arms and her pleading face was only inches from his—the world went black again.

For two days, he came and went, with her holding him steady to stand up and vent his bladder. Then she'd lead him back to the bedroll. Devils chased him through his hellish nightmares, and he wondered why she didn't leave him to die.

He awoke in a cold sweat and the stench of his own body odor assailed his nostrils. For sure he needed a bath. But the mountain fever had passed and he knew he'd recover quickly. Knotted muscles all over his body complained, but he knew that too would evaporate.

"Well, you look awake for the first time. Tell me," she said, walking over to stand above him with her hands on her hips. "Where in hell have you been?"

"You guessed it." He swept his too-long hair back with his fingers. "Whew, that was the worst session I ever had with the mountain fever in a long time."

"Worried me. But I'd worried a lot more if I'd known you probably were hanging on for your life to the saddle horn the last mile of that climb up here."

He smiled for her. "Thanks to you anyway."

"You rest. I found a spring on the way up here to water the horses and get drinking water. Tomorrow I'll get you down there for a bath."

"Sounds exciting enough."

She waved a finger at him. "You don't need nothing exciting yet."

"Damn my luck." He struggled to his feet and looked around. They were in a pine glen surrounded with graze for the horses. Good, she wasn't camped on the trail, but their experience of almost being discovered by the pack train taught her that. Hell, he'd come up there to find out about Apaches and he'd lost enough days to have found an army.

She took him around the waist, her hip to his legs, and hugged him. "It's been an exciting trip so far."

"Damned if it ain't."

That evening they were drinking coffee, seated at the small fire as twilight engulfed the mountains. He heard something and then his world went blank.

When he awoke, it was cool and dark. Must be close to dawn. The fire was dead. He knew he was alone. Listening as he could, there was no sounds of horses at sleep.

Whoever knocked him over the head must have taken her and their things. Who in the hell was it? Apaches? Outlaws? It would be dawn before he could read any signs. But he knew Apaches would have killed him. Especially if they knew who he was. He represented General Crook. That would be reason enough.

There were lots of bands of outlaws hiding in the Madres. This was a hard country to find a man in or even a gang. But an even tougher land to find anything to steal. Most of the resident denizens were living hand to mouth. His horses and the supplies would be a nice treasure, plus an attractive blond-headed woman. *Sumbitch.*

He felt his boot top. He still had his small .30-caliber Colt. Good, he wasn't defenseless. That could count for a lot in this vast range. He'd need to find her before the horny bastards wore her twat out raping her. What a damn mess. Maybe one of the pack mules got loose on them—he'd be around there grazing when the sun came up. At this point even a burro would do.

In the starlight penetrating through the pines, he found his saddlebags that they must have missed. In them was some jerky in the pouches as well as caps, bullets, and black powder for the .30. That was better than good news. It made a wonderful discovery for him.

Daylight finally came and the footprints were not Apaches. They'd ridden on east. Maybe four or five of them with all of his horses, mules, and Willa. They'd rue the day they'd done this to him and her. At least he felt strong enough to take up their trail.

By late afternoon, he could smell wood smoke, and began to take care as he approached the source. He soon discovered a wood cutters' camp and with the saddlebags slung over his shoulder and the .30 caliber revolver stuck in his waistband, he walked up to the site. Some women looked up in shock from their cooking.

"*Mi amiga.* Hold it. I am looking for some men that took my woman and horses last night before they rode by here. Have you seen them?"

"*Sí.* They are *bandidos, Señor,*" the short woman said to

him as the other two stood back, anxious-looking enough about his appearance to hug each other and act ready to run for the edge of the pine forest around them.

"I know they must be. What are their names?"

"The main one is Leon Silva. He is very mean and those others I don't know." She glanced back at the other two women as if questioning them and they shook their heads.

"Where does this Silva live?"

"I don't know—but he is a very mean man and rapes many women."

"Did he rape you or any of them this time?" He gave a head toss at the two girls.

She shook her head. "Our men were here and they had guns."

"Where are your men now?"

"Cutting wood on the mountain. If you listen you can hear them working. Would you have some coffee, Señor?"

"Yes, I would. I'm sorry, my name is Slocum."

"Mine is Renee. Her name is Sally, the other is Lou. This woman they took is your wife?"

"She is very important to me."

Renee nodded. "They did not waste much time here. Our men all had their guns ready."

She handed him a steaming cup. "Here. How will you catch them on foot?"

The other two became braver, he noticed, and joined her. "Can you ladies sell me a horse?"

They searched each others' faces. At last Renee said, "We have one that is not well broke."

"How much for it?"

"It will buck."

"I know buck. Is it sound?"

She glanced at the others and they nodded.

"May I see it?"

"Sure." She gathered her skirt and led him to a corral.

The short-coupled red roan mountain horse looked stout enough.

"How much?"

"Fifteen pesos."

"Is there an extra saddle?"

"It is old, but two pesos will buy it."

"Seventeen pesos. Is that enough?" He had that much money hidden in the vamp of his boot.

She looked at them for the answer, and they nodded woodenly.

"Yes, it is."

He removed his left boot and paid them from the money he recovered from the vamp, putting the rest of the small roll of bills in his pocket. "*Gracias.*"

They brought him an old bridle, a well-worn Indian blanket for a pad, and a very old wooden horn saddle. The girths looked all right. He went in the pen and caught the horse like he considered him well broke, brought him over on a lead to the saddle. Roan snorted at the pile, but Slocum ignored him trying to shy away from there. Holding him close by the makeshift halter, he forced him to smell the pad. That was soon on his back. Next he tossed up the saddle. Roan should just as well get used to it. When the saddle hit his back, Roan squatted down like he was going to toss it higher than the moon. No chance. In a flash, Slocum had the front girth hooked on him, and soon the latigoes were threaded in place. Drawing them tight made the horse roll his eyes around in their sockets. This would be a fun ride.

His nostrils flared, blowing snorts like rollers out of his nose, he was beginning to look like the he-devil that Slocum expected to be for sale in this remote camp. Never mind, he had to use what was available. He swung in the saddle in one fluid leap and checked the spooked young horse, then put his rein hand forward for him to go on. Stumbling over his feet the first few steps, Roan about went to this knees. Recovered, he half reared, then dove forward, kicked at the vacant air behind his rear hooves, and the war was on.

The first few jumps weren't too bad, but the horse gained some power, soared higher, coming down on all four feet. Then he sucked back and whirled a hard allemande left. Still not rid of his rider, he left out in short-coupled crow-hops. Slocum forced him to run, whipping him from side to side with the reins. The gelding tore down the trail like a racehorse, and finally Slocum reined him to a hard stop.

His shoulders lathered in sweat and gasping for his breath, the horse danced on his toes through the tall pines. And Slocum held him hard in check with the bridle. This pony would be better rode down some. All he needed was for someone to stick to him—but this could have happened at a more convenient time. Thing to do next was find the outlaws and rescue Willa from them.

By midday, he found where they had camped the night before. There he stopped and watered his horse. A good drink from the cool spring for himself and a jaw-bite of tough jerky made his meal. Back in the saddle, he short-loped on the trail that went around the mountain he was traveling on.

Late afternoon, he drew the sorrel down from the ground-scoring trot. Something was ahead beside the road. He pushed Red into the trees and made hobbles for him from some cotton rope he found in his saddlebags. Red secure, he set out on foot using the big trees for cover and occasionally seeing a bright bay horse fretting around a big pine where he was tied.

There could be a lookout for the gang up there. No other reason for anyone to stop. The next water source was over a half mile farther on. Silva might not be taking any chances.

Besides, he could use the guard's weapons and his horse.

With stealth he tried to stay out of sight. Ravens saw him and crowed about it. No way to do anything about them. Squirrels chattered about the invader, and a woodpecker quit beating his bill on the ponderosa bark when he drew closer.

The man, he discovered, was sitting up with his back to the trunk. His sombrero on the ground beside him. Was he asleep? Might be, but Slocum couldn't take a chance of him warning Silva. Surprise was his best advantage, and the long gun across that boy's lap would be another if he could get to the rifle and not be discovered.

His concern for Willa's safety became more pressing as he drew closer to the lookout. Then, pistol in his fist and the hammer cocked back, he bent over and put the muzzle in the guard's face. With his free hand he lifted the hexagon barrel of the .50-caliber rifle and set it against a tree.

"Silence, *amigo*. That is how you will live to fuck all the *putas* in Sonora and the rest of Mexico. Stand up." The wide-eyed boy scrambled to his feet. Slocum poked the .30 in the youth's muscle-hard stomach and jerked open his gun belt buckle with his left hand. That undone, he slung the holster set over his shoulder.

"Now why shouldn't I cut your throat?"

"I-I-did nothing to you."

"What about stealing my woman?"

The youth shook his head. "I never touched her, Señor."

"Get on your knees."

"Don't kill me. Mother of God, I never touched her."

He shoved him down, holstered the small revolver in his waistband, cut the rope that the boy wore for a belt, then used the cord and bound his hands behind his back. He wadded the youth's kerchief for a gag and then shoved him down on the ground. Without the rope belt to hold his britches up, the halves of his brown hatchet ass were exposed.

On the saddle horn of the glossy bay gelding were two

bandoliers of .50-caliber ammo. He took his time to lengthen the stirrups and then relace them. The .50-caliber buffalo gun in the scabbard, the Colt and holster hung with the ammo and the boy's sombrero, he swung into the saddle and went back for Red. Ammunition was no longer a problem. The long gun had a terrific range, and he might pick them off at a great distance with it, if the shots didn't endanger her.

Silva's camp, he soon discovered, was set in a green grassy basin with live water splashing through it. Horses and mules grazed down the valley and two small boys tended them. There would be no way get his own horses back.

Women toiled over a large campfire with kettles boiling frijoles or black beans. Some of them squatted beside a skillet making tortillas with their palms. No sign of Willa. But he felt certain this was where they held her. He checked the sun time—siesta time. The men must be napping under the ramada shades of canvas stretched over frames made from ropes tied to large trees.

Good, a few rounds well placed would wake them. He loaded the rifle and took aim at an unattended steaming kettle. The bullet exploded the iron pot. Hot water and beans flew everywhere. Screaming women and children fled the camp and ran toward the horse herd.

He ejected the empty casing and smiled as the six-gun-armed, half-naked man with a black mustache came charging out of the shade looking everywhere.

"Silva!" Slocum shouted.

"Where are you, *bastardo*?" The hairy-chested one shook his fist in the air.

"Drop you gun, or die."

The man raised his arms with the gun still in his fingers.

"If you want to live, tell all your men to come out and sit on the ground."

The six-gun still in Silva's raised fingers, Slocum figured he was considering his chances of living if he made the wrong move. Obviously, the shot into the kettle had made him cautious. Certainly he was thinking this man could shoot him and others before they could reach him.

Silva dropped his revolver.

"Now tell every man to come out and sit. I only want one thing today. I want my woman back. No one will die. No one will be hurt. But if I don't get her, I will kill five or six of you before you can get in range of me. Savvy?"

Silva waved at him. "I will tell my men to join me and I will send a woman after her."

"Don't be long or try any funny tricks. You'll die first." Sweat poured down Slocum's face, and he dried his hand on his pants every chance he dared. One man came out and quickly sat down, then another. Finally, seven men sat on the ground at Silva's feet.

"They are all here."

"No tricks. I can drive nails with this rifle. Send out my woman."

"No tricks."

Then Slocum saw a man with a rifle taking aim from the right of the largest shade. Slocum lifted the rifle, took aim, fired, then watched the man throw his arms up and fall over backward. Hit hard. The bullet aimed for Slocum raised dust thirty feet downhill from his position.

"Who else wants to die in your camp?" he shouted, his anger growing by the minute

"It was a mistake. A mistake. The woman she is coming," Silva shouted from his place on the ground in the cluster of men. He waved his hands in surrender.

There better not be any more of that or Silva would be wearing a coffin. Slocum saw Willa waving and starting for him. He wanted to ride down there, pick her up on horseback, but then he wouldn't have them held at bay. She'd have to make her way on foot up the steep hillside by herself.

Why was that other woman coming up the hillside with

her? They were halfway up when Willa dropped her shoulder and threw her elbow with all of her weight into the woman's chest. The victim fired off a cocked gun in her left hand before she went ass-over-teakettle in a show of white petticoats tumbling down the mountainside.

"I'm coming, Slocum. I'm coming," Willa said, out of breath, struggling up the steep face.

"You're fine. You're fine." He watched the men in camp—none moved. Obviously they expected some repercussions over their attempt to send a woman with Willa to shoot him.

"I couldn't signal you that she—she had a gun." Sucking in wind, Willa looked tired, but appeared relieved to be with him.

"Our horses are in the woods behind me. A sorrel and a bay. Get to them, I'm coming."

"What are you going to do?"

"Scatter their horses," he said under his breath. He swung the rifle around and took a shot at the feet of two grazing ponies. The rifle roared and dust flew in the horses' faces. They wheeled around. The herd heads flew up panicked. And then they stampeded down the valley despite the young tenders on foot trying to turn them back.

He reloaded, making sure that the men had not made any moves. "We will meet again, Silva. Don't try me unless you have confessed to a padre in a church."

"You are lucky, *amigo*. Next time I won't leave you alive."

A large earthen jar sat to their left. He took aim upon hearing Willa and the horses coming. The roar of the massive gun echoed down the canyon. Black powder smoke swept his face. The vessel exploded and threw water all over the outlaws' heads.

Good enough. He shoved the rifle in the scabbard and mounted Red. "Let's get the hell out of here."

"How did you do this?" She rode side by side with him.

"There's the reason." He pointed as they swept by the bare-assed guard with his hands still tied behind his back, stumbling along toward the camp.

"Where's his pants?"

"It's a long story."

A real long story—whew.

9

The village of San Tomas sat wedged deep in a canyon watered by a good-sized stream. Small irrigated plots lined the winding road, with patches of alfalfa, corn, and beans plus other garden varieties like onions, chilies, and tomatoes weighing down vines with great red fruit. A place where children, chickens, pigs, sheep, milk goats, and cows had a voice in the noise created between the high walls.

The strumming of a guitar invited Slocum inside a cantina that sat atop a tall flight of stairs. Inside, a blind man sat on a tall stool on the small stage and sang Mexican lost-love songs in a voice with such power that he made the skin crawl on Slocum's back.

". . . you will my lover, tonight." He ended with a hard ringing strum of the guitar strings.

"Did someone come in? I saw a shadow too big to be another fly passing through the doorway."

"I did." Slocum stepped over from ordering a beer at the bar to shake his hand. "Slocum's my name."

"Joaquin Johnny, they call me. You are a big man, Señor Slocum."

"Compared to what?"

Joaquin laughed. "An elephant perhaps."

"Perhaps."

"Do you come to look for the gold, Señor?"

"No, I came to swap an Indian out of a white girl."

"An Apache?"

"Yes, do you know any with a white woman captive?"

"Apaches think that I have powerful medicine. They can't understand I don't need my eyes to make music. Yes, I know some."

The man's mostly white eyes were distracting to look at. Slocum could understand why he disturbed the superstitious *Denay*. Things that were different or unusual about an individual bothered native people. He knew of a blue-eyed Indian who said his mother hid him from the others until he was four years old. He said that she believed they would have killed him otherwise

"You make good music. Make some more, but if you find an Apache I can talk to, let me know." He dropped two ten-centavo pieces that rang in the cup.

"You are very generous sir, for ten centavos I would sing for a long time. For two, maybe forever." Joaquin laughed and began to strum his guitar. "I shall look for that one."

Slocum went back and sipped on the beer, listening to the man sing a love song about a woman who waits for her man. The *cerveza* wasn't cold, but it was cool and cut the dust in his throat. The glass empty, he nodded at the bartender and left, going out the open doors and down the long flight of stairs to where Willa sat her horse and held his reins. "You learn anything up there?"

"You hear the singer?" Slocum tossed his head at the music and remounted.

"Yes."

"He's blind. He says he is special to the Apaches and will try to find one of them to talk to me."

"How did you do that in such a few minutes?"

"Our spirits crossed."

"Something crossed." She shook her head to show she doubted him. "Where will we stay?"

"Dona Valdez's place."

"What is it?"

"A whorehouse."

Willa looked to the blue skies for help.

He reached over and clapped her on the shoulder. "Don't worry, you'll like her."

"Slocum, have you ever taken a woman to a whorehouse before?"

"No, don't guess I have."

"Silly, you don't take them to one, you go there to find one."

"Wait. You have never met Dona Valdez."

"I guess then I'm going to anyway, like it or not."

He gave her a you-will sort of look and they rode on.

How could he tell her that these places in such remote country weren't like the whorehouses in Tucson or Tombstone. There the customer picked out a girl in the parlor, marched upstairs with her, had his privates washed off by hand in some hot soapy water until his pistol was cocked. Then his pecker and balls were dried off briskly, he jumped in bed and bang, it was over. Sorry, no seconds. But she'd learn all about the situation up there while he tried to find Whey or the Chiricahuas that held the Salazar girl.

Thunder close by told him that they needed to get on to the house of ill repute. He set his horse in a trot. Looking upset, she rode beside him.

In the cold rain pelting down on them in the courtyard, a barefoot boy came out to take their horses and Slocum sent Willa ahead. Soaked to the skin, she was not hard to convince to go on. At last, he guided her through the doorway and into the alcove with tile floors and tall ceilings that opened to the large living room.

Two young women, holding up a blanket, were asking her to undress there in the hallway. She frowned at him from behind the blanket's screen. However, she began to disrobe from her wet clothing. Then they wrapped her in the mountain-woven-cotton blanket and the shortest one hurried her down the hallway.

"Well, look who the rain chased in," the taller one said, and flipped her shoulder-length black hair back from her face as she held the second blanket up for him.

"Yes, a drowned rat."

"No, Señor." The she looked around with a mischievous set to her lips. "Did you think there were no women here and brought your own?"

"No, I rescued her from some *bandidos* in the mountains," he said.

"Oh, I only wanted to tease you. Now undress. Already you have drained a lot of water on the floor."

"I see that."

He shed his knee-high boots—the hardest part. Then he hung his gun belt over her head and one shoulder. The rest came off quickly, until he hesitated at taking off the bottom half of his underwear. She again laughed out loud at him.

"If I had a big dick like that one of yours, I'd show it off every chance I got. They're wet, take 'em off."

"This dick on you? Why, they'd for sure all want to see it." He hopped around on one foot, then the other, taking the wet sticking bottoms half off.

The young woman holding the blanket up to cover him when he was through was bowed over laughing. "I bet they would."

She delivered him to a large bedroom, where he found Willa dressing behind a Chinese screen.

"*Gracias*," he said to the girl and closed the door. "This is better than being in a stable."

Willa came out in a fluffy robe and nodded. "I agree. Only what do I charge?"

He swept her up in his arms, then bent over and kissed her. He could taste her mouth—the sweet nectar had not left her, despite, no doubt, the outlaws' attempts to defile her. They finally parted and she buried her head against his chest. "I thought I would be with them forever. That they'd killed you and no one would even know where I was at."

"I know. I know." He rocked her in his arms. "I can't make what happened go away. All I can do is try to make today and tomorrow better."

"I want a bath before we do a thing. I want every stinking drop of them off my skin."

"I understand."

A knock on the door made him realize he was naked. He grabbed the blanket and she cracked the door.

"They have hot water for a bath," Willa said over her shoulder.

"Let them in. That's what you ordered."

"I ordered?"

"Yes, you said—"

She threw open the door and three women marched in with two pails apiece. They looked amused at him wrapped in a blanket. Then they dumped the hot-smelling contents of their containers into the copper tub.

"We can bring rinse water later," the one in charge said. "Pull that velvet cord when you want some."

Willa frowned at the rope hanging beside the door against the wall. "*Sí*, I can do that."

She bolted the door after them. "Are these people mind readers?"

"Some of them are."

She undid the robe, slipped out of it, and then put it on a

straight-back chair. Her pointed full breasts jiggled as she bent over to test the temperature with her hand. She straightened and sight of her long white shapely derriere brought back tantalizing thoughts of sessions they'd shared connected.

"A little hot, but that might be good. It will erase more of their marks."

The blanket off her, he stood by holding the long-handled brush.

She laughed at his pose as she cautiously stepped into the tub. "Are you in a hurry?"

"No. You're setting the time."

Submerged so her breasts floated, she smiled. "I won't be long."

"Good," he said, and moved in to scrub her back.

She closed her eyes at his attention and acted as if she was in another world, gripping the edge of the tub as he worked the brush hard up and down her spine. Amused, he applied lots of effort to his handiwork. Then he bent over and kissed her mouth.

When he straightened, she slumped down in the water and slowly smiled at him. "Pull the rope."

Later, they sat together at the large table in the kitchen with the handful of women who worked there and ate a great meal of barbequed goat, roasted ears of corn, beans, rice, and fresh fruit. Introducing them to the others, Dona sat at the head of the table in charge.

The dark-eyed woman still held her youthful looks and figure. Behind her mysterious eyes Slocum felt there rested a real *bruja*. But her witch qualities had always been to his advantage.

"What brings you to San Tomas?" she asked.

"Willa was kidnapped and being held by Leon Silva and I took her back from him."

Dona nodded like she understood. "A very dangerous man."

"Were you afraid dealing with him?" one of the doves asked.

He nodded. "I am always afraid messing with such cut-throats."

Dona shook her head and spoke to Willa. "You must be very strong. Oh, I would have died from fear if they held me hostage."

Willa put down her fork. "Trust me, I was very afraid."

"Let our guest rest," Dona said. "She has been though some very trying days. Our good *amigo* Slocum regained her freedom and he is the hero of the day." She clapped, and the others did too.

He nodded in acceptance. "The important thing is she is safe now."

"He is so hard a man to pin his bravery on," Dona said and smiled.

Later the stable boy came by and brought him a message. Joaquin Johnny wanted to see him. He excused himself from Dona and Willa's company in her quarters and went for his horse. The storms had cleared out, and stars danced in the heavens. He rode his horse down the rock-based road. His hoofbeats rang loud in the night's stillness, the only sound save for some crickets.

Joaquin's voice wafted out of the well-lit cantina when Slocum dismounted at the foot of the long stairs. Several horses and saddled mules were at the base standing hipshot in the night's darkness. He tied his with them. At the top of the stairs, he paused at the open doorway to let his eyes adjust to the light inside. Several vaqueros were dancing around the floor with women in short skirts. Often, their hands slipped down to pat or feel a bare leg under the hem. Tequila and mescal freely flowed. The women grew loud and noisy; the men were full of *oh-la*'s to their flirting ways. *Mucho* fiesta time in San Tomas.

The bartender smiled at the sight of Slocum when he found his way to the bar through the crowd.

"A beer," he said, and the barman nodded.

"Who are you, gringo?" a short, sharp-featured man next to him asked with a slur in his words.

"My name is Slocum."

"Mine is Benito. Welcome to San Tomas, hombre. You want pussy tonight you must wait in line. On weeknights, twenty centavos would buy the best one in here for all night. On Saturday night, they want a peso for lying on their backs for such a short time." He held his index finger and thumb barely apart. "Then they want more money or get your ass out."

"I'll wait till then." Slocum took a sip of the foamy cap on his glass.

"Me too. Why is it that women have all the money in the world?"

"I don't know."

"'Cause they got all the pussy." Benito laughed until he cried. "You savvy, hombre, they have all the pussy too."

"I savvy." The music had stopped and Slocum excused himself to go speak to Joaquin.

"Ah, Slocum, you got my message." Joaquin must have recognized something he heard.

"What did you learn?"

"Ken'yah was here today. She's a young Apache woman. I asked her about the white woman. She said she would check for me and be back on Wednesday if the *federales* weren't here then."

"They come often?"

"No, but they do come here sometimes."

Slocum put a peso in the cup.

"*Gracias, mi amigo.*" Then he motioned to his musicians

that they must go back to work. "I will send you word when she gets here." He put the guitar strap back over his head.

"*Gracias*. I will be at Dona's."

The man nodded and began to strum his guitar to the loud shouts of hurrah. A short woman jumped off the bar where she was seated, and before she could push her turned up skirt down, everyone looking saw her hairy cunt. A night to howl at the moon. They were getting it on in San Tomas.

Slocum recalled having sex with a woman in an alley during a fandango in Santa Fe. He asked her if she remembered who all she had treated to her body on such a night, and she laughed. "Hell, darling, I will always remember your big cock."

He'd of bet she'd soon forgot him, because sure enough, not twenty minutes later, he watched her take another big *bastardo* by the arm and head him for the alley. So went the fickle-hearted woman of Latin blood's generosity during a fiesta.

The patrons in the cantina had a too-good-enough start on getting drunk for him to start in with and enjoy one's self. He slipped out the door and smiled to himself at the man who was bent over licking some gal's bared tits. Both were so far out of it, he'd bet that they never even noticed his departure down the staircase.

On his horse at last, under the stars, he headed back to Dona's.

In the courtyard, the boy took his horse and he thanked him. He could see Willa on the porch sitting in a swing.

Standing before her, he removed his hat and wiped his forehead on his sleeve. The night air was cooling fast. Then, with a smile, he accepted her offer of a seat beside her.

"Did you find a lead on her?" she asked.

"Joaquin says there is an Apache woman who might help me."

"Where is she?" Willa put her arm on his shoulder when he slumped down in the swing.

"Oh, she's from their camp in the mountains. She's due back here midweek if the *federales* don't come."

"Will they come?"

"I don't think they have a schedule, but Joaquin says they don't come by—often."

"What do we do until then?"

"Tonight?"

"Oh, that too." She laughed softly.

He smiled at her. That was the first time that she'd laughed since he recovered her from the bandits.

She raised up and kissed him. "I'm ready."

"So am I."

He listened to the night insects and let her pull him to his feet. Maybe he was close to finding a way to retrieve the Salazar girl. Arms around her, he spun her up against him. "Let's go wear out the mattress."

"Yes," she said in a smoky voice. "I can't hardly wait."

10

The next morning, Slocum drank coffee with Dona in the kitchen. A rooster crowed in the yard. Besides the two girls working in the spacious room preparing things for the day's meals, they were the only ones up.

"The woman with you is very strong." Dona sipped her coffee, but her dark eyes never left looking at him.

"Very strong. She's fought Apaches."

A smile parted her full lips. "I know, she told me. She said if she'd ever got hold of his pistol, Silva would be dead now."

"Shame she didn't reach it."

"Yes, he is no good and bad for the mountains. He preys on the weak."

"Why don't the *federales* take him out?"

She looked at the ceiling. "Maybe he pays the right people."

"Ah, the political. Yes. I understand."

"This is a poor district. A politician has a hard time extracting enough money from the people up here. So a bandit like Silva pays him protection money. The *federales* look the other way, huh?"

"I see, my lady."

"Do you think you can get that young woman away from Whey?"

"For a price. Yes. There are only a few of those bronco Apaches left. The U.S. Army will soon get permission to come over the border and Crook will sweep down on them."

"Do they know that?"

"Yes. They would much rather be held by the Americans than be in Mexico's prison and mines. Down here the Apaches would be wasted. In the U.S. they might survive, and they know that too. Giving the girl back might weigh easier on the great white father when judgment day comes."

"So time is the answer, huh?"

"Time. Yes. I'm more concerned about my contact getting here." Slocum hunched his shoulders against the tight muscles.

"Who is that?" She placed the mug back on the counter.

"A young man who's supposed to be my guide and the source of any money I'll need to pay for her freedom."

"What's his name?"

"Estevan. In the mess with Silva kidnapping Willa, I forgot all about that he is supposed to catch up with us."

"Where could he be?"

"Damned if I know. Oh, he'll show up. He knows the mountains and he's half Indian anyway. Besides, he's really a *pistolero* for the Salazar hacienda."

Dona laughed and reached over to squeeze his arm. "How do you get in such messes like this one? Who else could they hire to try and get some white woman out of an Apache camp? It is crazy."

"I guess I am crazy too."

"No. No. You are a good man. It is my own people who have lost their minds. This *bandido* Silva runs around like he reigns over these mountains. What help is our army?"

"I have no idea."

"None."

Two hours later, one of the kitchen girls came rushing in the house, out of breath. "The *federales* are coming!"

"Where are they?"

"I saw them and their horses at the cantina."

Slocum, who had been resting in a hammock, came into the kitchen and joined the war cabinet. "How many?"

"Maybe an entire company," the blanched-faced girl said, mopping the sweat from her face.

"What does that mean?" Slocum asked Dona.

"There is trouble is my first thought. They usually only have an officer and six men." Dona rose and began to pace across the kitchen and back.

"What should I do?"

"Stay put. We will see who is the officer in charge. If I know him you are fine."

"What if you don't know him?" Willa asked, coming in the room drying her hair.

"Then we go to another plan."

Everyone laughed, but Slocum could tell it was an anxious laugh.

"Then I'll go back to sleep," Slocum shook his head and started outside. "You girls figure it all out. It sure means the Apache woman won't come into town and trade."

Two hours later, an officer and four soldiers rode in the courtyard. From his hammock, Slocum could hear them talking.

"Ah, my lovely Dona."

The man in charge talked precise Spanish. He was not from border trash. He told his men to stay there.

"Captain Hernandez. Welcome to my poor *casa*." Dona headed him off at the front doorway.

"I must talk to the gringo who is here."

"Ah. Señor Slocum."

"Yes, yes."

"What is wrong?" Dona asked him as they came toward the kitchen.

Slocum took his place at the back door.

"Ah, you must be the one called Slocum." The shorter, stiff-backed officer began removing the fine goatskin glove off his right hand. "They tell me you know everything goes on below the border."

"I don't know about that," Slocum said.

They shook hands, each took up a stool, and Hernandez sat across from him. "What is General Garcia doing?"

"I don't know."

"They tell me he has a cannon and several troops assembled."

"I know nothing about the troops. A week ago, I did see some men transporting a caisson to the north."

"Where was this?"

"In the desert, way west of the Madres."

"What in the hell is he up to, do you know?" Hernandez frowned at him, looking deeply upset.

Slocum shook his head. "I thought he was on maneuvers for you."

"No."

"Is that why you are here?"

"To find you and try to find out what he was thinking. The U.S. Army didn't hire him, did they?"

"No. Crook wants his hands on Geronimo, Whey, and the rest of them so bad that he would do nothing to upset the Mexican government, I can assure you."

"That makes me feel much better. *Gracias*." Hernandez looked relieved and forced a smile. "Why are you here, if

I may ask? Of course anyone entertained by the lovely
Dona—"

"Whey kidnapped a friend of mine's daughter. I want to
try and get her back—alive."

"Are you sure he has not already eaten her?"

"Don't mention that." The notion disgusted Slocum.

"Well, the man is a cannibal among other things."

"What about Garcia?"

"If he isn't working for the U.S., then he must be setting
himself up for a revolution."

"I was with General Crook ten days ago. He has no such
plans. He's even watching the border so no guns can get in
to them or the Apaches."

"Where will you go next?"

"If I get her free, I'll be out of here."

"Could I hire you then?"

Slocum shook his head. "I don't make a good spy."

"You have military experience with such a weapon, no?"

"Yes, and I say stay away from the range of that damn
thing."

"How far?"

"Half a mile."

"That is what I thought. I must go now. Your information
is very informative. *Gracias, señor.*"

"Wait. Let Crook send some men and army scouts down
here and he'll end this Apache war."

"I will talk to my commander."

"Do that. We don't want Sonora. We want to stop this
border crossing and put them on reservations."

"Good luck ransoming her. I must go now."

That was good news, the sooner he and his trooper left
the village, the quicker this woman might come back.

"Good day, Captain."

Slocum strode to the front door and saw them off. The
man wasn't such a bad sport for a federal academy graduate.

He might even be fun to team up with and do a few skirmishes with. There Slocum went again looking for more to get into.

Slocum decided there was a sign out in front—SLOCUM IS HERE. In the afternoon Estevan showed up, his horse on its last legs, and he looked like he'd been dragged through a knothole.

"What have you learned?" the man asked.

"Leon Silva whacked me over the head and kidnapped Mrs. Malloy."

His eyes flew open wide. "Where is she now?"

"In the kitchen eating something."

"Is Silva still alive?"

"Today, yes."

"What about Estria Salazar?"

"We are waiting on an Apache woman to come to town to find out what she's found out."

"Dona, meet Estevan. The guide I have waited for."

Dona smiled looking him over. "After you eat, we will ready you a bath. And if you like, someone to cut your beard."

"I'd like both. Señora."

"You can have both."

"You remember Willa?" Slocum asked him when she joined them.

"*Sí*, good to see you, Señora Malloy."

Later after lunch, in the midst of Slocum's siesta, one of the kitchen girls knocked on Slocum's door to wake him and give him the news some boy brought to the *casa*. He was needed at the cantina. Half asleep, he strapped on his six-gun.

"I'll be back," he said to Willa.

Sitting up holding the sheet in front of her nakedness, she frowned. "You need me?"

"I imagine I will only talk some more. I hope that Ken'yah is there to tell me something."

"You be careful."

"I will."

At the cantina, he dismounted at the base of the stairs, hitched the horse, and took the steps two at a time. Inside, the bartender gave him a head toss toward the back. Slocum thanked him and crossed the empty barroom. He parted the curtain and let one of the saloon girls out, then walked down the narrow dark hallway headed for the back door.

"Slocum?" Joaquin called out, and the man appeared in the last door.

When Slocum stepped inside the narrow room, he saw an Apache woman sitting on the cot and nodded to her. Then he noticed another person huddled under a blanket—who was she?

"This is Ken'yah," Joaquin said, taking a seat on the chair.

Slocum nodded. "What does she know?"

"She wants some money."

"For what?"

"For the return of the girl."

"How much?"

"How much do you have?"

"Fifty dollars right now is about all I have on me."

"I think she would be satisfied with that much. Pay her."

"Where is the girl? Is she all right?"

Joaquin nodded toward the one in the corner and then he spoke to her. "Estria, this man will get you home safely."

The girl under the blanket threw the cover back. "Do you know my parents?"

"Sí. I am certain they will be very pleased to see you." How did he get her back this easy? His daddy always said never look a gift horse in the mouth, accept it and run like hell.

All the paper money he had on him he placed in the woman's hands. She nodded. "This will feed the children."

"Good. Keep the blanket cover on," Slocum said to Estria. "I don't want anyone to recognize you. My horse is at the foot of the stairs. Then we will go to a safe house, and when it is all clear I'll take you home."

"That would be very nice."

"Joaquin, what do I owe you?"

The singer shook his head. "You don't owe me a thing."

"No. Señor Salazar will pay you well for this." Slocum nodded in gratitude to Ken'yah, and then he guided Estria toward the door.

In the hallway, he turned back and asked, "Where is Whey?"

Both of them shrugged—hell, for all they knew, he could be around the corner of the cantina. Time to use his brain. He must hide her until he could get her safely out of the mountains.

"I am going to hustle you down the stairs and to my horse. Keep your head covered. No one needs to see who you are."

She nodded. He went to the back door and looked around at the bare ground. His spine tingled. One word, one shot were things he did not need. The girl didn't look too wrought up about her captivity—some lost their minds after being repeatedly raped and abused. A strong young girl—but regardless, she was many miles from home.

Many dangerous ones too.

11

The tracks the two of them made going through the near-empty cantina were swift ones. He saw she wore some Apache moccasins and she could move. But outside, he worried she might tumble down the stairs at the rate they were taking them, but he kept a firm hand on her shoulder to steady her.

At the base, he boosted her in the saddle like she was a feather, undid the reins, and swung up behind her. They were gone in some hard cat hops uphill, and him hoping all the time that her identity was hidden under the blanket.

When they reached Dona's house, he swung down and then caught her in his arms. "Go in the front door. You are in a safe place."

He looked around the courtyard. Soon, the stable boy came on the run and took his horse. One more check—nothing, and he followed her in the front door.

Willa came running across the tile floor of the great room. "What—who is she?" she whispered.

"Estria Salazar, meet Willa Malloy."

Dona, her skirts and petticoats in her hand, came running in from the other direction. "Is this her?"

Slocum nodded. "We have her. Now to get her safely home."

"Ah, Señorita," Estevan said coming in the room. "How are you?"

"Fine," she said as they peeled her out of the hot blanket. "Good to see you again, Estevan."

There was some restraint in her words that niggled Slocum, but the girls were already preparing to take her off for a bath and some clean clothing. So they didn't like the smoky squaw perfume she wore. He never minded it.

The notion reminded him of the Apache girl called Cry, who nearly screwed him to death one night under the giant walnut tree in the dry wash between Fort Bowie and the Butterfield stage station. Cry had muscles in her pussy that could squeeze a man harder than a powerful man's fist. Whew, she wore that mesquite smoke perfume and it took three hard fought rounds on top of her, bang, bang, bang, to even make her eyes swim in the moonlight as she lay underneath him.

His depleted balls ached for days after that occasion. The thing she whispered in his ear the next morning before dawn, he'd never forgotten. "Only thing better than you is a stud horse I know about . . ."

Then in a soft swish of her many skirts, she pulled them on over her shapely legs and tied the strings at her narrow waist, and in a flash she was gone in the shadowy light. He never saw her again. Though he'd looked over many of the women at San Carlos, Fort Apache, even Fort McDowell. Never did he find Cry again. He spoke to a few Apache scouts about the woman, and they were amazed that he knew her. She was legend, but they didn't know where she had gone either.

The two women were going out of the room with Estria,

leaving like noisy magpies and herding their ward with them. Good, she needed some tender care after all she'd been through. Those two could give her such tending.

"When do we leave for the hacienda?" Estevan asked.

"Shortly. I don't want everyone to know who she is."

"Her parents are very anxious to have her home again."

"I know that. But my concern in this case means how do we get her back there without confronting any more Apaches or bandits. The four of us would stand little chance against any such force in these mountains."

"How did you get her anyway?"

"The Apache women needed food for their children back in camp. One woman brought her to me. I paid her fifty some dollars I had on me."

"Is that all?"

"It was all I had."

Estevan shook his head. "Fifty dollars. That's cheap."

"You owe that blind singer Joaquin at the cantina a couple of hundred. He arranged it. I had no money left for him."

"I'll see they pay him."

"Good."

Slocum poured them both some of Dona's good whiskey in small glasses and raised his in a toast. "Here's to getting her home."

"Yes, getting her home—safely." They clinked their glasses.

Willa finally returned and took her place on Slocum's lap. "She's sleeping now. That poor girl has been through a lot."

Estevan nodded. "I imagine so."

"She asked about her fiancé. Do you know him?" Willa asked him.

"Ah, Felix Francisco." Estevan shook his head to dismiss the notion of him. "She won't need to worry about him. He gave up on her the day he heard that the Apaches had taken her—" Then he lowered his voice. "And they'd popped her cherry."

Willa made a face of disapproval and then shrugged it off. "I guess men do that."

"A man would be foolish to do that to such a fine woman," Slocum said with a frown.

"Ah, you don't know this man," Estevan said. "He thinks so much of himself, he has no room for anyone else. She is better off without him."

"Yes, but she must have had some attachment to him or she'd never asked," Willa said.

"Those are rules she lives under. A man chosen to marry her is her husband-to-be or was. I think he's near bankruptcy and only came into her life to save his own backside. You know the patron, her father, he is very rich. She is the only heir to all his ranches and mines. I think the patron thought Francisco was the man to run his businesses when he passed on. But he's only a horny womanizer who expected to pluck a flower on his wedding night."

"I guess being a *pistolero* for such a man, you know lots that goes on?" Willa asked,

"Security is my business."

Slocum stood up and stretched. "I'm going to take a siesta before supper."

She jumped off his lap and pulled him up. "There is plenty of time for that."

"Estevan, you keep an eye out. I'll do guard duty tonight. I don't think anyone knows much right now, but the rumors will fly."

"I can handle it."

"Good." Slocum pushed himself out of the deep chair and with his arm over Willa's shoulder, they went off down the hall, talking softly to each other.

"How will we get out of here? Not that godforsaken hogback trail I hope?"

"We'll have to go the best way that we can find."

She ducked and looked back to be certain they were alone. Satisfied acting, she turned around and under her breath spoke, "What does he know about popping her cherry?"

"I'm not certain. Something's going on there. Her coolness toward him was obvious when I introduced them. I may have to send him on a wild lark if he's going to be a problem to her."

"And where was he all that time he was supposed to be catching up with us?"

"Good question. I better find out from her exactly what is going on."

Willa nodded and opened the heavy door to their apartment. A stiff breeze was coming through the open French doors and thunder rumbled in the distance. An afternoon shower was teasing the mountains. Soon cold breaths of air swept into the room, and goose bumps popped out on the back of her arms as he rubbed them, facing her.

"Let's get in bed and under the covers." She shuddered and hugged him, her face on his chest.

He toed off his boots. She fussed with the strings that held her skirt on. He hung his gun belt on the ladder chair. With a knowing wink at her, he shed his pants and hung them on the other corner of the chair. Her shapely white legs exposed, she reached upward and shed her blouse, exposing her pointed breasts that quaked. Vest, shirt gone, he spanked her fine derriere as he climbed up onto the high feather bed and followed her.

Outside, the wind rustled through the garden, tossing small debris around and rattling the rose bushes. Far away, some horses whinnied as the storm drew closer. He was braced over the top of her, her knees wide spread and his growing erection against her flat belly.

With a grin, he bent down and sampled her mouth. Honey on his tongue never tasted any better. She reached between them, raised her butt enough, and inserted his dick in her gates.

A brilliant blinding flash and thunder crashed so loud, it rattled large pots in the courtyard. The report covered her sharp cry when the head of his throbbing dick passed through her ring of fire. Then the grumble rolled on and on forever as he eased his turgid tool in and out of her. Rain tore at the plastered adobe walls like her hands that clutched him, then raising her butt off the bed to meet his thrust. More wind whistled in the eves outside. Water ran off the tile roof and crashed on the walkways in torrents.

The storm and their lovemaking went on and on until he felt the swelling begin in his testicles, and then two arrows shot him in the butt and hot lava exploded out the end of his skintight cock.

She let out a sigh and collapsed, looking up bleary-eyed at him. "Stay in me a while longer."

He agreed and propped himself up so as not to crush her.

Outside, the small birds had returned to chirping and the sunlight soon shone—the violent storm had gone on—but not before watering Dona's flowers and garden.

"Where will you go after we return her?"

"I have no great idea. Right now I'm in your trap." He winked at her.

She wiggled to stretch under him. "I could keep you right there forever. But I know someday you will have to go help Tom Horn or George Crook."

"Yes, someday I'll have to leave. Deputies from Kansas are after me. Sooner or later they'll come looking."

"Will the army tell them where you are?"

"Not Crook's staff, but talk's cheap at a fort. You get a few soldiers drunk and they'll tell you the secret details."

She began to work the muscles and hunch against him.

"Let's do it again. I've got an itching needs scratched in there again."

He went back to work.

At supper, Estria told them that food was a short commodity in the Apache camp. While the people could live on little—they had nothing, especially with their men gone on hunts and even battles that produced little game meat.

"I think they are very tired of war," Estria finally said.

"But men like Whey and Geronimo won't let them quit, will they?" Slocum refilled his glass of wine.

"That is true. Those two keep seeing dreams where the white man leaves much like he did in the Civil War. Only now, the dreams are the white man goes in caves. They seal the entrance and the white man can't ever come back."

"How easy to get rid of your enemies." Willa passed the meat tray.

"Only they believe it." Estria shook her head. "The one thing I learned—they are very content to live in grass huts and under canvas shelters. And with little food, few personal belongings. Ken'yah pawned her Navajo silver turquoise necklace a few weeks ago for a sack of frijoles to feed them. I asked if that hurt her, and she shook her head. 'Better my belly does not cry than my neck.'"

Slocum agreed, forking more meat on his plate. "They don't want things better or even more peaceful. This is how they have lived for centuries. At war with everyone. They ran the poor Mexicans out of their northern provinces and controlled it with how many? A few hundred warriors?

"There couldn't have been many more than that." At last Slocum put his fork down, his stomach so full he thought he might explode. "The food was very good tonight."

Everyone agreed.

Estria excused herself, and Dona told her to go back to the room and rest.

The girl paused and held onto the top of the high-back chair. "I am so grateful for your hospitality and all the dangers you have faced coming after me. I am certain that my father will pay all of you for your work in my behalf."

"I will see to all of that, Señorita," Estevan said.

"Very good. Be generous," she said to him.

He nodded.

12

Later that night, past midnight when the others were in bed asleep, Slocum roamed outside the house in the starlight with a Winchester in his hands. Listening to the wind, he tried to imagine who might try to come for her. Finding her was one thing, getting her out of the Madres another.

The afternoon shower had dropped the temperature, so he wore a serape to turn off the chill. He rested on one of the benches that encircled the trunk of a great old oak.

"Señor?"

He twisted to see the shadow of her figure wrapped in a blanket in the dark doorway and nodded. "Yes, what can I do for you, Estria?"

"I couldn't sleep." Then, tightly wrapped, she came barefooted across the flat rock laid for a sidewalk. "Who sent this Estevan after me?"

"Your father's man, I guess. He was supposed to get the ransom when I found out the amount and bring it back to me. Why, don't you trust him?"

"No. I—I once had an affair with him. I was much younger then and he was not much older."

"How did that turn out?"

"You can imagine, can't you? Him a common *pistolero*, me the heiress to one of the richest families in Mexico."

Slocum smiled as she leaned forward and huddled in her covering. "He said he wanted me. Now, who knows?"

"Was he the first one?"

She blinked at him and shook her head, looking like she wondered why he asked. "No."

"He says your fiancé left after the Indians took you and they broke you in."

"Good, I don't need him anyway. Francisco is such a donkey ass who my father thought could run our family business and would make me a good husband. Frisco thinks he's a lover and lady killer." She wrinkled her nose. "He has a small dog's dick, need I say more?"

"No. What should I do about Estevan?"

"Nothing for now."

"You give me a sign and his ass is gone from here."

"You may need him. We all may need him to even get out of here."

Slocum agreed. "Good night, Estria."

"Good night, Señor."

A short while later, satisfied there was no immediate problem, he undressed, then crawled in bed to discover Willa's silky bare warm skin under the covers. His hands ran over her nakedness and she rolled on her back to face him with a sleepy "Yes" escaping her lips.

"The Apache didn't get her virginity and neither did Estevan," he whispered in her ear.

"How did you find that out?"

"We talked tonight."

"Who took it then?"

"She never said. But not the Apaches or Estevan."

Willa laughed out loud. "Our little lady is no helpless thing."

"No, she isn't."

"Was it you who popped hers?"

"Not guilty." He leaned over and kissed her hard on the mouth.

Recovering her breath, she gouged him in the side. "Pop mine then."

"I can do that."

And he did.

He slept till noon, then bathed and shaved. If he didn't move quickly, from this point on he'd draw trouble like a dead cow at a water hole drew flies. Estria would need a good horse—Estevan could go find supplies and pack animals and could handle that chore, too. He'd need to hire three or four tough men. Joaquin would help him do that. And they needed to leave in the morning.

Slocum found Estevan in the great room. They sat at the end of the dining table and discussed their needs. Willa joined them.

"We better plan on two weeks' supplies for eight people," Slocum said.

"Eight?"

"Yes." Slocum knew he was figuring long, but better that than be short. "I intend to hire some men to ride with us."

"But how will you know—"

"I'll get men who you can buy their loyalty—today."

Estevan shrugged. "So much to pay for in so short a time."

"Add some extra saddle horses too. By dawn, with or without things, we ride out of here."

"*Sí.*"

Estevan immediately left for town.

Willa nodded when he was gone. "What part is he playing? The loyal *pistolero*? Or something else?"

"I think he wants a chance to win her back. But I doubt he turns her head. She considers her affair with him as an inexperienced mistake the way I get it."

Willa nodded.

"I must go see Joaquin and find some men."

"I'll ride along and hold the horses."

"Tell Dona we'll be back. I'll go get my rifle just in case."

She agreed.

In a half hour, they were at the cantina. Slocum left Willa with the horses at the base of the stairs. He was in the cantina talking to his blind friend at a corner table.

"Four men, I know I can get," Joaquin said. "They may need rifles. They are not boys and would be tough under fire."

"I can get them rifles. A hundred pesos per man."

"For that much money you could hire a *generale* from the Mexican army."

"Just so they are at Dona's casa before dawn."

"I'll tell them to bring their horses in case your man can't find them."

"Yes. I'll add fifty a man if they ride their own."

Joaquin whistled. "Four men will be there before dawn—that you can trust."

"*Gracias, mi amigo.*" They shook hands and Slocum left the cantina to hurry down the stairs. She was already mounted and handed him his reins.

"The deal is set?"

"Yes, ma'am. We will meet them in the morning at the casa."

Estevan lived up to his duties to return with horses, mules, and supplies in the packsaddles. Willa went over the list of things he'd purchased. He lacked the four rifles, so Slocum rode back and bought them—two were used, but both had been well cared for—and several boxes of cartridges. His armory's cost was put on the charges to the Salazar hacienda. Thank goodness their credit was good in Sonora. He rode back and handed them one at a time to Willa, who came out to greet him.

"I see you have it all. We will be like an army, huh?" She took the last two long guns from him and set them against the wall.

"We'll deliver her anyway."

"Do you expect much trouble?"

"I am simply preparing for it."

"Yes. We'll be prepared."

Estria joined them, sweeping the wave of dark hair back from her face and looking over the courtyard full of horses and mules. "You go to no small expense."

"It's your money. It's my job to get you back there."

"Oh. Slocum, I appreciate all you have done for me."

"When you're back at the hacienda, you must see that the bills at the store is paid. Plus, the blind musician Joaquin and Dona as well."

"I will take care of them and be certain they are paid."

"Good," he said. He noticed for the first time how drawn she looked—the Apaches' lack of food had no doubt taken several pounds off her that she didn't have to lose. Back home, she'd recover quickly, but that sanctuary was perhaps two hundred tough miles away.

His people were busy feeding the mules and horses when Dona joined them.

"One thing I shall leave you," Slocum smiled at her. "Plenty of horse manure."

"It will be fine. We can pile it out behind the stables for the fall garden plantings and the rain will wash the rest away."

"We'll be out of your hair in the morning."

"You have never been in our hair." Dona hugged his arm. "I love Willa. She would be a good woman for you to settle down with. I know. I know. You think you can never do that. But others have vanished before you."

"We do thank you." He wanted off the business of talking about him settling down. That remained an impossible task he was not prepared to face—no way could he settle under any roof with those relentless deputies on his heels.

"Still, we are grateful," he said.

"Come by when you are near here, or just come by. We all love you here."

"Thanks again."

"I better go see about supper. We are having a feast tonight. You will love it."

"Always. Always." They parted and he went to see about a mule's hoof that the stable boy had noticed.

After examining it, he assured the young man it was only a small hoof crack and shouldn't hurt him. Then he went on to the house to wash up. He passed Estevan in the hallway and congratulated him on his excellent job of gathering it all in so short a time.

The man acknowledged his words and excused himself. He had things he must do.

Slocum went on, washed his hands and face at the bowls and towels set out for the task. Feeling some refreshed, he went in the great room and took a glass of wine that Willa delivered. Hard to fathom, he'd be on the road with all his train at this time the next day. Damn.

In the morning, he met the four new men in the lamplight. Cordova, the tallest of them, maybe five-nine. Trevino, the oldest, with some gray in his hair when he removed his sombrero and shook Slocum's hand. Diego, the youngest, but also the hardest-looking, and Jimenez, the round-faced burly one with a big smile.

"If no one told you," Slocum began. "We are going to the Salazar hacienda and deliver his daughter Estria to her parents. She was taken captive some weeks ago by the

Apaches and we ransomed her from them. They may try to take her back. I have had words and trouble with Leon Silva and his band of cutthroats coming in here. You know there are more gangs of bandits than that. Our job is to avoid any trouble and get Estria home as quickly as possible. You savvy greed, right?"

"*Sí.*"

"We have to prevent it."

They nodded. Willa handed out rifles and cartridges.

"We will ride out in thirty minutes. Who is the best scout?"

"Trevino," the other three said.

"Trevino, you leave now and scout ahead. We will join you at the Gap."

"Ah, *sí.* You boys can tend those mules." He mounted up and slapped his short coupled mountain horse on the butt with his rifle to make him get around. "Señor Slocum, I will meet you and the train at the Gap."

Slocum waved to him and he was gone. Good, he had an advance lookout. Boosting Willa on her horse, he helped Estria too. Her in the saddle, he noticed she was crying in the candle lamplight.

"Don't cry now. It will be all right."

"But I will truly miss my new amigos and Dona."

"So will we." He clapped her on the leg and went to see about the rest. Twenty minutes before first light, they filed out. He was the last to leave the courtyard, and waved to Dona and the crew as he rode out.

Mules complained. Fresh horses sidestepped in their impatience to move along faster. One of the hired guns was using his quirt on the stubborn pack mules that tried to lag. Soon, they learned that to hesitate would get them busted, and any rider coming by was enough to make them tuck tail and lunge forward.

Estevan rode in the lead and the two women with him. Slocum had assigned Willa to be with her—the men could drive the mules. Two jerked lead ropes, the other one made them trot. They soon were through the sleeping village and headed up the steep mountain trail.

The canyon swallowed them as the first light shone behind the peaks. Slocum knew he'd feel less jumpy if they were over this pass. Any attempt to stop them, or take her, could be set up in this area as they climbed into the taller timber. He had to trust Trevino's six senses. But the men had voted him as the best—it was their necks also that could be chopped off.

Bare hooves clapped on the rocks. Iron shoes clanged on the small pathway. Animals grunted and strained, saddle leather creaked. They'd be to the top in another hour. So far so good. But it could never last. Standing in the stirrups, he passed the train and joined the women and Estevan.

"You all are making it?" Slocum settled his horse into a trot with theirs.

"So far, but we aren't to noon yet," Willa reminded him.

"We'll break about then. There usually is adequate graze in the Gap. We need to kind of baby this stock. There won't be much graze once we reach the desert floor. We'll buy grain where we can for them."

"Do you think anyone will try to get at us before we get out of the mountains?" Willa asked.

"If I knew that I'd avoid them." He glanced back. The mules and riders were doing fine.

The two women nodded.

By noontime, they reached the wide meadows and made camp in a defensible place in the pine timber at the edge. The campsite was close enough that they had access to the spring that fed a small watercourse, which filled the animals. Mules rolled on their backs in the dry grass and dirt to satisfy the itching of their hides.

Slocum noticed the clouds were building. They could use a rain. They were about fifteen miles from Dona's and that much closer to the Salazar hacienda. It would take two weeks to get there—but he had plenty of time if the bad ones left them alone. But Mexico was a desperate place— bank robberies netted little money in many places. The robbers found the safes empty. Men were killed in alleys for less than a dollar in change. So his cargo was plenty valuable, and no mistaking sooner or later someone would try them.

The two women cooked food. The men on horseback dragged in some hardwood for their cooking fire. Trevino and Slocum sat on their haunches and discussed the trail they should take in the morning going down in the foothills. Estevan was off scouting in a wide circle to look for any sign of a threat. Willa soon brought the two men cups and a pot of fresh coffee.

The older man doffed his hat to her, "*Gracias, Señora.*"

"So you think the Stone Canyon is the way off?" Slocum winked at her and nodded approval as she poured his cup full.

"*Sí*, the other trails are exposed in the open, but it is twenty miles by Stone Canyon till we reach a good place to camp. It will be a long day in the saddle."

"There are some strong springs to water the animals along the way." But it held a big danger that concerned Slocum. "A flash flood up here could wipe us out in that canyon. Maybe by the time the showers start in the afternoon, we will be far enough down to get away from them." Slocum blew on his coffee.

"We could leave in the night and be out of the canyon by afternoon."

"Good idea." The coffee was rich-roasted and Slocum was enjoying each sip. "We will tell them the plan at supper."

"I'm going to take a siesta."

Estria met Trevino and gave him something wrapped in flour tortilla. Then, with a pan in one hand and her skirt in the other, she carried one to Slocum. With Estria stopped, standing over the top of him, he swiveled on his toes and looked at the wrap in the pan.

"It is dried apples, brown sugar, and raisins."

"No poison?"

"No poison." Then she laughed aloud at his question. "Why would we poison you?"

"I was only teasing you. *Gracias*, you two will spoil my men."

"It wouldn't hurt them," she said, ready to go back.

"I am glad to see you laugh." Slocum held the warm tortilla in both hands, all fixed to taste it. The fumes of the apple's tart sweetness and cinnamon tickled his nose.

She stopped and looked back at him. "I am glad too. I thought I forgot how to do that."

Good. In a few weeks, perhaps when she was at the hacienda, she would return to the normal girl that the Apaches had kidnapped. He hoped so. At the first bite, his mouth flooded with saliva. Ah, something from heaven to eat. Willa was behind this dish—she certainly knew how to cook. Such a good woman. He knew many, all of them special, but she was out of the ordinary. Never acted jealous or pouty, and shared herself with the men and the girl. Even Dona had noted her good temperament, and after all of Willa's concern about the house of ill repute, the place was no problem for her to live in.

In late afternoon, his men gathered in to dry. An afternoon shower peppered the canvas shelter they'd thrown up and their roof was being pecked at by small hail and large cold droplets. Squatted and sipping the coffee in their cups, the men agreed to the notion that to be far down Stone Canyon by mid afternoon the next day would be a good idea and the safest one.

Thunder cracked and rolled across the Madres in blinding displays. Rain ran off the edges and down the hillside.

The thirsty soil sponged the moisture up. In a week the grass would be green again across the meadow. At last, the passing storm let up. Then another batch of clouds moved over and soaked things down again. Off and on until the sun went down, streaks of rain came across them.

They were eating her bacon and frijoles when they heard a horse coming hard up the back trail. Hands went for gun butts, and two of the men brandished their rifles.

Slocum rose with his plate in his hand. "Easy, boys, he could be friendly."

"It's the stable boy, Baca, from Dona's." Willa, holding her skirt up, ran to meet him. "Baca, what's wrong?"

"A—bandit—has shot her. *Mi* Dona."

"Which one?" Slocum's eyes narrowed in the twilight." Who would do such a dastardly thing?"

"Is she all right?" Willa held the boy's arms.

"No—Señora, she died."

"What is his name?" Slocum demanded.

"Silva."

"Oh, you poor boy—" Willa smothered him in her arms. The boy cried on her. With her mouth drawn in a tight line, she asked, "Why did he do that?"

"I don't know. He was drunk. He was angry. I was so afraid. He swore and shouted about Slocum a lot."

She turned back to Slocum. "What should we do?"

"Kill him," Slocum said in a hard-sounding voice. "But first Estria must be in safe hands."

"The closest place is your friend, Lou Valencia's hacienda."

"Yes, and that's three days' hard riding."

"Then we'd need fresh horses to ride back. And it would be a week later."

Slocum nodded. No matter, Leon Silva did not deserve to live a day longer. The nerve of that bastard to kill such a

dear woman was beyond his wildest consideration. And
Silva's men were no better for letting him do it. Damn, they
all needed to be sent into hell's hottest fire forever.

They loaded up after only a few hours' sleep. The men
acted numb, but that was only from lack of sleep. They'd be
a lot sleepier than that before they reached the Valencia
hacienda.

By late afternoon they swept out of Stone Canyon, watered their horses at the mission, and put feed bags of corn
on the mules' and horses' noses. They ate food from some
street vendors and after dipping their bare heads in the horse
tank, replaced their sombreros and rode on.

The desert brought heat, which fatigued them more.
Dead carcasses lined the road, some of the hide still on
them and they looked fierce. Dead horses' skulls showing
bared teeth with a coat of dusty hair on their cheekbones
became creatures from another bad world. He'd never
really noticed the dead before—under the hot relentless
sun, they laid among sparkling diamonds.

Slocum made certain all their mounts were steady at the
next watering hole. More grain was fed them. Their noisy
chomping went on as Willa and Estria distributed jerky to
everyone.

They slept a few hours down the road and were up ready
to move at sundown. One mule had taken the shakes and
stood trembling under his packsaddle. It would not move
despite the men cussing him.

Slocum saw they'd never do anything with him, rode in
and stopped them. "Get what we need off of him and put it
on the others. He won't be any good to us."

"Damn mule anyway," Cordova swore.

"We're lucky there isn't more like him." Slocum spurred
his dull horse back to the head of the line.

"How much farther?" Willa asked under her breath.

"A day, I hope. How is she?" he asked.

"Sick to her stomach. She'll be all right."

"Anything wrong?"

"No, but we hope everything is all right."

"What do you mean?" He frowned and pushed his horse in close to hers.

"That she doesn't have his baby in her belly. Her bleeding may start today."

Good heavens, he had never even thought about that.

13

They reached the hacienda past midnight. Guards had raced ahead to wake everyone. The house was lit up and Lou was out giving orders.

"You found her!" Lou shouted at Slocum, who dropped heavy out of the saddle and then stood to get his legs steady with his hand on the spent trembling horse.

"We got her back. That damned Silva shot a good friend of mine after we left the village."

"I'm sorry."

"He's the one's going to be sorry. I want four or five horses to go back. I'm going to sleep a few hours, then you need to roust me."

His host frowned at him. "You aren't going back—so soon?"

"In the morning. Yes, I want Silva put away once and for all. He kidnapped and raped Willa. I should have shot him then when I got her back. Maybe Dona would be alive if I had."

"Marty, show him and his lady to a bedroom," Lou shouted to a woman.

"*Sí, patrón.*"

Estevan carried Estria in his arms over to them. "She just fainted. I asked her how she was and her knees buckled."

"She'll be fine," Slocum said, exchanging a confiding look with Willa.

She nodded and they went to the house with the woman Marty.

No need to undress, they flopped facedown across the feather bed and instantly went to sleep. A noisy rooster woke him and he wondered where in the hell he was at for a few seconds. Valencia's hacienda.

"I'm goin'." He shook her, backing off the top of the bed.

She moaned and he combed his hair back through his fingers looking down at her. Damn, she'd sure be pissed if he left her. "Come on. We're leaving."

Weakly, she waved him away, nesting her face deeper in the goose down. He nodded and strapping on his holster, he went through the doorway.

"Slocum you better wait for me," she shouted loud enough to rattle the glassware. Coming out of the room, she had one boot on and was one-legged hopping to get the other one on.

He leaned his back to the wall to wait. Damn, he was bone tired, hungover, and whipped, but Silva wasn't getting by with murder. Slocum and Willa walked outside and there were six horses saddled, and two pack mules.

"You men—" He looked over the four of them and Lou. They looked worse than he did. "I can get Silva, you men go collect your pay from her father."

"You forget," Trevino said. "Dona Valdez was damn sure our friend too."

"Estria will be fine here," Lou said. "I have sent for Salazar to bring a carriage and an escort for her return. Salazar will pay. To have his daughter back he would give his fortunes."

With a nod, Slocum let the stirrup leathers down to better fit his legs, something he'd intended to fix for days. Willa did the other side. Six against those bandits was better than one or two. He closed his dry eyes—what a helluva mess. But he knew Estria was safe in more ways than one.

They gnawed on jerky and jog-trotted their fresh horses eastward. In two days he wanted to be at the base of the Madres. That evening, squatted in the dust, they ate with a street vendor. The wizened old lady cackled and told them dirty jokes about her days as a *puta*. Slocum doubted anyone that ugly could even have coaxed a bad drunk to climb on top of her—who knew anyway. After he paid her they rode on.

"Even her food was lousy," Willa said, riding beside him through the narrow streets. "And her jokes weren't funny either."

"You laughed."

"Someone had to."

Slocum chuckled. "You're right. Let's shuck this village and find us a place under the stars."

Standing in the stirrups, they left in a long trot. Eventually, out under the stars and a short distance from the road, they hobbled their horses and each threw down a ground cloth and a blanket. Desert heat evaporated quickly in the night and with a kiss, he rolled over and went to sleep.

The next morning, Cordova told him about a small *rancheria* at the base of the Madres where they could buy food and feed for their horses. "I would trust this man with my life."

Slocum nodded. "Let's make his place by tonight."

Cordova looked satisfied. "We can do that."

Midday, Trevino pointed to some dust on the northern

horizon. Slocum agreed and thanked him. Might be the general moving things again. He wished he had time to at least see who it was, but they had a course to follow. They'd made good time so far. The horses were holding up, and by afternoon would see the mountain peaks on the horizon.

Let the general alone. Silva was his goal.

Plato Maderia was a short man who lived under a palm-frond-roofed ramada with a young pregnant wife and three small ones. His teeth shone and he removed his sombrero to bow for Willa.

"Welcome to my humble house, Señora," he said. "We can butcher a goat and have him cooked in a short while."

"That would be good," she said. "These men are full of jerky. I can help."

"But you are—"

"I am no princess. You butcher the goat. I can make tortillas and fix some frijoles."

"Eva will help you."

"If she is strong enough."

"She is a good woman."

Willa agreed and Plato went off to get the goat.

Two of the men chopped mesquite for the fire; the others put feed bags on the horses and mules. Slocum watched the operation, pleased that Cordova knew of this place. In the morning they'd attack the mountains. The horses were still fresh enough. But then they had to find Dona's killers. The job would be a tough one. People hid outlaws for money. Others had relatives in the gang and owed loyalty to them.

Willa had mentioned there were ten of them. She obviously knew them well enough from her abduction, and he'd made a mental list of each one she'd told him about.

Ortega, the number two
Tonto, the crazy one

Ferdinand, the fat one
Paulo, the kid
Santos, the knife man
Pedro, the horse man
Frank, the quiet one
Carlos, the redheaded Mexican
Devaca, the short one

His plan was to separate and divide them. As a gang they would be tough. As individuals he could learn what they knew. His plan was to catch them away from the others and one by one eliminate them.

"What are you thinking?" Trevino asked, squatting beside him.

"There are ten main men in that gang. Do you know them?"

"Some of them."

"They kidnapped Willa, you knew that?"

"Yes, we learned that on the trip to the hacienda."

"So we need to find them one by one away from the camp and eliminate them."

"Ferdinand?" Slocum asked the older man.

"He's the fat one. He has a small rancheria and a young wife. He spends lots of time there when he can." Cordova and the others had joined them. From their nods it looked like the *fat one* would be first.

"He is the one that cut my brother's boy's throat," Diego, the youngest, said. "They did it just to be mean. The fat one, he accused Miguel of messing with his wife. The boy, who was younger than me, had never even saw her. He cut his throat in front of Miguel's poor mother."

"We will start with him," Slocum said.

"He shot two vaqueros in the back who were traveling through and then he sold their horses and saddles."

Slocum had heard enough about this bad one. Before they left, he gave Maderia five dollars for feeding them supper and breakfast plus horse feed.

"*Gracias*." He turned his palms up. "I would go with you and help you punish them. But my next one is long overdue, and you see I have children to help her with."

"No problem. I have some good men to ride with me." Slocum nodded to the man and rode off after the others.

They entered the Madres undiscovered and made a remote camp. Then Slocum took Cordova and Trevino with him to find the first one. Ferdinand was at home, taking a siesta in a hammock. It was no problem to slip up on him. Several feet away from his hand hung his sidearm and holster. He would regret that mistake, Slocum felt certain.

Cordova put the loop of his lariat on the snoring outlaw's left leg. And then they ordered the half-awake prisoner on his feet. Ferdinand acted mad when they asked him where his boss was at.

"You sonsabitches ain't getting nothing out of me. I ain't afraid to die."

"Good," Trevino said and shoved him out of the yard. When Cordova returned with their horses, he took the tail of the rope from Slocum.

"Has he told you yet where his boss is at?" Cordova asked, dallying the rope around the saddle horn.

"No," Trevino said.

Cordova leaned on the horn and looked hard at their prisoner. "You ready to tell us where he is?"

"I'll see all of you in hell first!"

With a wary shake of his head, Cordova turned off his horse and then gouged his sides with the spurs. His drag-behind began to scream bloody murder bouncing over brittle sagebrush and through a patch of prickly pear. The small horse dug in hard to sling him on a roll into another cactus bed. At last, in a begging voice, Ferdinand asked for them to stop.

Crying and his face full of spines, he lay on his back moaning when Slocum and the old man walked up. "You're killing me."

"Where's Silva?" Slocum asked, ignoring his pleading. This man never gave others any comfort.

"At—his—ranch."

Slocum turned to Trevino. "You know where that is?"

The older man tested the edge of his large knife on his thumb. "Yes, we know where he has one.

"You remember a boy named Miguel that you cut his throat in front of his mother?" Trevino bent over and grasped a fist full of the man's dirty, dry-weed-entangled hair to raise his head up.

"Yeah."

"Good, then you know how you will die."

"No!"

Trevino bent over and silenced him with a zip of his super-sharp knife from ear to ear. Cordova nodded in approval, then stepped down, undid his reata, and coiled it getting back on his horse.

"Who is next?" he asked.

"Silva. Without a leader, they will be uncertain," Trevino said.

Slocum agreed. If any of the others escaped, he wouldn't worry about them as much as he would if Silva got away from them.

"We better leave the others in camp and get Silva next." They mounted up and headed for the outlaw leader's ranch. Trevino led them.

Using field glasses, Slocum scanned the place from the high spot above the ranch house. Three big brindle cur dogs were loose around the house. He counted the curs getting up to go piss on something, then going back to lounge around the front porch, snarling at one another and at the rest of the world.

"Those damn dogs may be a problem," Slocum said, giving the glasses to Cordova.

"Naw, I can go down there and lure them away and kill them."

"I'd like to see that." Slocum had his doubts.

"I'll show you how." Cordova grinned big.

"But if Silva gets word—"

"You are right." Cordova rose and brushed the dirt and twigs off his shirt front. "I know what those dogs need."

"What's that?" Slocum asked.

"Some goats to eat."

"How do we get them?"

"Goats are easy to catch." Cordova went for his horse.

"He'll get some," Trevino said, like it was nothing.

In a short while, Cordova was back and had two young goat carcasses with their throats cut. He nodded and set out on his horse for the house. Cordova stayed out of sight and downwind. The dogs soon caught the goats' scent and ran to get them. Still under the hill and out of sight from the house, he began to drag his bait behind the horse at a lope. Snarling and fighting with each other, the curs tried to catch his bait and tear a bite off the flying goats.

Slocum heard three muffled shots and then no more dogs snarling. Cordova came back shortly—still no sign of anyone around the place.

"Did you see anyone come out?" Cordova asked, taking a position beside them on his belly.

"No, we watched close. I had the .50-caliber ready."

"I don't think anyone is home."

"Wait," Trevino said, holding his arm out. The man used the glasses and then handed them to Slocum. "She must have been sleeping through all this."

Slocum caught a glimpse of a naked tan body standing on the porch. Her lithe figure was one of a young woman and her long black hair swayed like willow tree limbs in the soft wind. He heard her clap her hands—but no dogs came. She went to the edge of the porch, bent over, and peered around the corner for them, giving him a bird's-eye view of her shapely ass. Then standing straight again, she cupped her pointed breasts and threw her head back as if in a lover's control. Soon shaking her head, she went back inside.

"I don't think he is there."

Slocum saw a rider coming hard from the south on a fine barb horse through the junipers toward the house and corrals.

"That is him. It is Silva," Trevino said. "That is the horse he stole from Don Carlos."

Silva dismounted and looked around like he too wondered where his dogs were at. Then his naked lover rushed outside and leaped in his arms.

"I guess she owns no clothes," Trevino said.

They laughed.

"Give him a few minutes," Slocum said, getting up on his hands and knees. "And we will take him by surprise."

"Good," Cordova said.

"Let's go. By the time we get there he'll be plowing her field." Slocum brushed himself off and then slid the big gun in the scabbard. They went through the timber, down across the grassy ground cut by a spring's flow, and up the other side to come in from the back side of the house. Moving catlike on foot, they approached the jacal, disturbing a brown setting hen who got mad and wanted to fight them.

They ignored her anger. Trevino missed kicking her to shut her up. All three of them with their cocked six-guns in their fists were looking all around the entire time as they drew closer and closer to the jacal.

Then they heard a scream from inside.

"You bitch! You tricked me! Where are my dogs?"

More screams. "I don't know. I don't know. One minute they were here, the next they were gone."

The sound of someone inside being slapped around and another crying out was louder as Slocum edged himself along the jacal's wall for a window.

"Who are they?" Silva shouted at her.

Next Slocum heard Cordova order, "Don't move."

Slocum rushed to the window on his side and saw inside that the naked Silva had a gun to her ear. "One wrong move and I kill her."

Terror in her brown eyes. Silva's left hand was full of her long silky hair and the six-shooter in his other. "I'll kill her. I'll kill her."

"Easy," Slocum said to his men.

"You better go easy," Silva said, backing for the doorway. "Stay right there. Stay there," he ordered, and then with his hair-hold, he drew her body against his own as a shield.

Suddenly, he was outside beyond the hitch rack, threw her down, and mounted his horse from the right side. Leaning on its neck to get his reins, he urged it on, clinging to the barb's far side. The horse raced away leaving Slocum and the other two without a target.

Upset over them missing him, Slocum hated worse that Silva knew they were after him.

"How did he know we were here?" Trevino asked.

"He has a guardian angel," Slocum said. He frowned, looking around. "Where's Cordova?"

Trevino gave a head toss at the front door. "He took her back inside. She was pretty upset."

The rascal. Slocum motioned toward the way they came. "We better go get our horses."

He cast a last glance back at the adobe hovel. They needed to bring more lightning pressure on all the outlaws and Silva. Maybe split the crew, have two attack units, perhaps then even a fortune-telling bandit couldn't know all about them. The cur dogs being missing must have cued Silva something was wrong. Slocum'd learned a lesson—don't underestimate Silva again.

They rode back to the hovel with Cordova's horse to get him. He came out grinning, tucking in his shirt and redoing his pants.

Slocum winked at Trevino. "I guess she's doing better, huh?"

Stopped, Cordova was ready to mount up. "Oh, *sí.*"

He swung in the saddle and they left Silva's ranch. Headed for the others who would be anxious to hear the results, Slocum also planned to move their camp so the outlaws couldn't surprise them.

Things were a long ways from going smooth, but they had one down and nine to go. He spurred his horse into a lope. He was anxious to share Willa's company and get his mind off this outlaw problem.

14

"What will you do next?" Willa asked him. Her warm skin, firm breasts, and sensuous body snuggled tightly against him under the bedroll's canvas cover.

Distant thunder growled at them. The last of the afternoon storms moved on. Only the drip off the pines was left to splatter on their shield.

"We'll cut out some more of his gang. Unless they den up in a fort, we will pick them off one at a time."

"What if they flee the Madres?"

He raised her chin and tasted the remains of honey on her lips. "We'll handle that too."

Soon they were lost in a sea of passion that swept them from the mountains to new heights in the towering clouds. He felt her firmness, teased her nipple with the pad of his thumb until it hardened, then they kissed until their breath expired. His hand slid over her flat stomach and soon ran over the patch of stiff pubic hair. Her knees raised, she parted them for him and closed her eyes to savor the pleasure of his teasing. Her breathing increased and she squirmed until at last she pulled on him to get on top.

He eased himself over onto her and then he kissed her. Moving hard toward each other, he probed in and out of her to the bottom, and then with her swept up in the whirling spiral of the process, she began to *oh* and *aw* aloud. The muscular walls of her vagina began to close in powerful spasms around his shaft. Soon he felt forces crush his testicles. He drove to the bottom of her well, and forced a fountain of his hot cum out of the swollen head of his dick. They collapsed in an exhausted heap and slept.

Dawn and he softened the whisker stubble on his upper lip in the steam off his coffee. Seated on the ground with the rifle over his lap, he listened and watched for anything out of place. A light fog, waist high, shrouded the large meadow where the horses were hobbled and grazing. Nice cool mountain morning. Some camp-robbing magpies were flitting around where Willa was preparing breakfast on the oak wood fire. Sharp-smelling smoke on the breath of the air stirred around her.

"Where will we go today?" Bent over her sizzling bacon, she threw her head up to look in his direction.

"Jimenez thinks Pedro, the horse man, might be at his home rancheria. You recall him?"

She made a cross look at him, then turned back to her cooking. "I will never ever forget a one of those bastards."

"I figured as much."

She glanced back at him and gave him a sharp nod. "Every damn one of them."

He'd not tried to learn much about her day or so spent in their camp. In time, he felt she would tell him all about them. And he didn't think being held as a prisoner had been any pleasure for her. But rehashing a real bad experience is not always the best thing to do until the person involved has sorted some of it out with themselves. Sounded like she was about ready to talk about it.

"You better wake up the crew. My gravy is about done."

He rose and went off to do that. Nudging each man in a bedroll with his boot toe, his crew was soon up yawning and stretching. He'd have to wait until later to hear her version.

"Things look quiet?" Cordova asked, looking about the camp.

Slocum nodded.

"Diego can stay here today and watch over the camp and her."

"I wants to go along," Willa said.

"Fine. I thought . . ."

"I know, but I want to see every one of these guys pay for what they did to me."

"I savvy."

After breakfast, they left Diego in charge and rode out. On the way, Jimenez explained that Pedro's place was no hacienda and they should not expect too much.

"I think he is the toughest of the bunch," the man said. "He has killed many men and done it in a bad way. He hung my brother-in-law by his feet in a well and when he could no longer hold his head up, he drowned."

Willa nodded that she agreed. "He's plenty cruel."

"That was Phillip's brother Juan," Cordova said. "That he did that to."

Jimenez agreed, though Slocum had no idea who Phillip was, but he listened to them.

"Juan was a good man too. He had children and a wife too."

"Why did he do such a thing?"

"He thought Juan was messing with this wife."

"Was he?"

"No, he didn't even know her."

"Who was messing with his wife?" Slocum twisted in the saddle and looked back over his shoulder—nothing back there.

"Many men—he never caught all of them. But Juan was not one of them. Oh, Pedro's wife, she was a *puta* and a *bruja* too."

"And she was mean as hell," Trevino said, sounding like he knew her as well, and then he laughed. "But—I am so sorry, Señora—but she was very good-looking."

"Don't worry about me, Trevino," Willa said. "I grew up around teamsters. I've heard every story they tell and some of them are tough, too."

They laughed a little easier as they rode on.

They found Pedro's place and from a safe distance, not to alert him, Slocum scoped the place in his field glasses. Sure enough, a woman was under the brush-piled-high frame, taking a spit bath.

He handed the glasses to Trevino and smiled. "I think she's home."

"Well, damned if she isn't. Her name is Roberta."

Cordova was next to look, and made a small whistling through his front teeth.

Jimenez had to adjust the glasses to see her and chuckled. "It's her all right. She has a spur scar on her right hip. I can see it. Some lover must of thought she wasn't going fast enough."

Willa took her turn and nodded. "I see why they gathered like buzzards at a dead cow carcass around a water hole. She is a very attractive woman even seeing her from here."

"Now we've all seen all of her, where's Pedro?" Slocum took back his glasses.

"He may be asleep."

"If we ride in, we'll put him on the defensive even if he doesn't know what we're up to."

"We can scatter out to surround the camp and then take him," Trevino suggested.

"Good idea. Let's be careful."

The men choose where they would come in from and they spread out to close in on the shade. Through the glasses, at last Slocum saw a good horse hitched almost out of sight on the far side of the property. That meant that Pedro was there and sleeping. He rose and dusted himself off. "Let's go eliminate one more."

She gave him a grim nod.

Then the two of them slipped along through the trees, keeping down and out of sight. To the east, they found a place where they could get much closer under cover. Then they had a stroke of good luck.

Groggy-acting, Pedro came from the shade with a handful of corn cobs and soon dropped his pants to squat down. He was grunting like a hog when Slocum rose with his pistol in his fist and came in behind his back.

"Don't move a muscle."

"Huh?"

"I said—don't—" Slocum heard someone fighting with his woman.

"I'll go see," Willa said, and set out in a run for the shade before he could stop her.

"Who are you, gringo—ah, the one with the rifle. What do you want this time?"

"Where is your boss? Silva?"

"At home I guess."

"No. He's not there now."

"I don't know."

"Maybe we can refresh your memory." Slocum could see Cordova was coming, riding Pedro's good gray horse. He undid the reata and threaded out some line to Slocum who motioned with his gun for the prisoner to move.

"Lift your foot," Slocum ordered.

Pedro raised his foot for Slocum to put the noose around his left ankle. Pedro walked out of the low sagebrush into the grassy area. The others were bringing Roberta down from the shade with her arms bound behind her back. If dark eyes would kill someone, she was trying hard to do that.

"Now start telling us who's in the gang and where they are," Slocum said.

"Fuck you, gringo."

"No, it will be you who gets fucked here. Either tell me or you face the worst interrogation a man can get."

"In—tero what?"

"Start talking now."

"Fuck—" That was all he got out when he realized that Cordova was wrapping the reata around the horn and gouging his big horse to ready him to go.

A scream came from Pedro's mouth and his bare feet flew in the air. His butt was hitting the ground every once in a while. Cordova fed out some of the rope so his victim was further back, and when he circled that distance, he swung the spinning outlaw farther out on the curve.

He raced down the meadow then turned the gray gelding back hard. That threw Pedro out in a wide arc and flying into a large bed of prickly pear, sending pads flying with him rolling over and over in them.

Then Cordova pulled him out into the open. He lay screaming, his face and body full of long cactus spines. Dismounted, Cordova shook loose his reata from his ankle and coiled it up. "Ask him if he remembered Juan, Jimenez."

"Do you remember drowning my brother-in-law?"

"No."

"You want to eat some more cactus?"

"No. No."

"What about it?"

"I—I did it. It was they—the—the thing to do."

"Where are the others at?"

"Fidela's place—"

Jimenez nodded to Slocum that he knew where that was at. Then he drew his cap-and-ball pistol, cocked it, and shot the moaning outlaw right between the eyes, with a "Go to hell, you sorry bastard."

The bound-up woman raced over, fell on her knees with her arms tied behind her back, and cried for him. "Mother of God forgive him . . ."

"Fidela's place is a cantina in a small village, not far from here. We can ride there tomorrow," Trevino said to Slocum. "We can get all of them then."

"I think Santos may be with his wife. I bet it's the single ones that are at the cantina. Let's go find Santos next," Slocum said, putting his arm on Willa's shoulder. "These guys can handle the rest here."

How did that go? To the victor went the spoils. Obviously, his three men had other plans for Pedro's wife rather than her lamenting about her lover's death.

The next one to see was Santos at his place. In a short while, Slocum's men rejoined them and they cut across country. Trevino knew the canyon where the outlaw kept a woman if he was home. Slocum and Willa rode down the canyon and the others came up from the base, so he would be trapped between them.

Slocum heard shots and nodded to Willa. "The SOB must have spotted the others." He jerked the .50-caliber Sharps out of the scabbard and swung down. She caught his horse's rein and turned him back. Then she sprinted them for the brush.

Slocum loaded the rifle. Then he saw someone come around the adobe hovel and stop; the outlaw looked shocked to see him, and took a wild shot at him, but the distance was too great for his pistol. The sight raised, Slocum cocked the hammer and took aim. Santos broke for the cover of a partially collapsed wall. But the huge slug caught him and threw him sideways.

The acrid gun smoke in his eyes, Slocum knew his target was down and wouldn't get up. Trevino came around the corner and waved to Slocum that it was over. The older man bent over, cleaning out Santos's pockets and taking the man's firearm.

"He won't cut anyone ever again."

Slocum agree. "Did he have a good knife on him?"

"No, they must be in the hovel." His man nodded and then shouted over his shoulder for the others to look for his good knives.

Jimenez soon came around with a large bowie knife. "This would tire me to have to use it."

"Yes, but it is made of special steel and would bring a good price in a real market," Slocum said.

"For the Madres, it is too heavy."

Willa even laughed. Slocum put it in his saddlebags and then stepped aboard.

They rode up on Fidela's place after dark. Music of guitars and fiddles carried into the night. Screams of wild women carried out into the night. Jimenez went around back to be certain the outlaws' horses were in the corrals and to make sure there was no way for them to get the animals out of those pens. He tied up all the gates.

Armed with all the weapons they had collected, each of his men had plenty of loaded arms. Slocum liked the idea. Firepower won wars and they had plenty. Five, maybe six outlaws could be in there raising hell with some half-drunk *putas*. This situation could be either easy or volatile as blasting powder. His forces divided front and back, he waited for Jimenez to come tell them the horses were locked up tight.

Slocum and Trevino took the front doors and busted into the saloon, guns cocked and ready. Cordova and Jimenez charged in through the back entrance. The *putas* screamed and dove for cover. Shouting in rage, a flat-faced Indian's shrill cries would have curdled most men's blood. He raced over, then tried to belly over the bar and get to a shotgun. Pistol shots cut him down and he ended on his butt on the floor at the base of the bar—dying.

"That's Tonto," Trevino said with a head toss toward the dying outlaw, disarming the kid Paulo.

"Where's Ortega?" Slocum demanded, dragging the midget, Devaca, out from under a table by his collar.

The wide-eyed dwarf threw up his hands. "How should I know?"

Slocum caught a dove by the arm and jerked her around to face him. "Frank?"

She gave a head toss, and Trevino headed for the curtain and the back cribs.

"Be careful." Slocum jerked her up hard enough she'd remember. "Where's Rojo, his name is Carlos?"

She drew back as if she was afraid he'd slap her. "He was not here."

There were more shots, and Cordova rushed through the curtains to see about them. In a few seconds he and Trevino were back.

"Frank is dead," the older man said, reloading his cartridge model Colt.

Grim nods around the room. The midget Devaca held up his hands in defense at his discovery that they were all looking at him. "Don't kill me. I'll do anything."

"We ain't interested." Slocum holstered his Colt. "Hang him and the kid."

Cordova caught his arm and jerked him out the front door. Slocum poured himself a couple of fingers of mescal in a clean glass and downed it. Then he slapped money on the bar. "Give me two bottles of your best."

"Sure. Sure, Señor," the bartender said to please him. Panic written on his face, obviously he feared they might think he was a gang member too and execute him.

Slocum took a bottle in each hand, motioned to the money on the bar. "That enough?"

"Oh, *sí*. Oh, *sí*."

Willa was outside in the night, sitting her horse, holding the reins for him at the base of the stairs. "Three left. Carlos, Ortega and Silva."

Slocum nodded looking at the short outlaw Devaca's and Paulo's forms swinging limply from the corral crossover bar under the starlight. "I've got us something to drink before we ride back to camp."

He held up the bottles and then dropped them to his sides. That worthless Silva was still on the loose. Carlos was a simple killer and they'd find him, but Silva had more lives than a cat. He'd be tougher than a dumb *bandido* to catch, but Slocum aimed to bring him to justice too. That left Ortega, his second in command, to round up.

Jimenez, Cordova, and Trevino with Slocum and Willa headed for the camp and Diego. The first bottle was opened and passed around on their way back to their horses. Then they mounted up and Cordova tossed the first empty one aside in a crash.

"Here's to those killers and the ones still alive," Trevino said.

Slocum slid the last bottle into his saddlebags. They were all drunk enough. He never could tell when they might be under the eye of that damn Silva. Damn, he was getting jumpy thinking about him. They'd get him. He'd slip up. Had he ever even been at the cantina that evening? They'd probably never know.

Silva might be a mile away, in the shadows of the night they rode through, waiting in ambush or miles away. The whole thing made Slocum itchy as they headed for camp.

"You guys have any idea where he might hide next?"

"He has many people in fear. They would hide him

afraid of what he would do to them and their family if they didn't keep quiet," Trevino said.

"I think he may try to get you," Cordova said, sounding a little in his cups.

"Why?"

"You have executed his gang. He will have to find more cutthroats or lose his hold on this part of the Madres. You've shown he is vulnerable. I think he will ride away and go round up more gang members."

"Where would such a man look for them?" Slocum glanced over his shoulder at the pearly light on the taller pines and the lower juniper brush. Nothing.

"The best—place—the border. Trash hangs close to there so they can slip either way and escape arrest from authorities on both sides, huh?"

Slocum agreed. There had to be an answer for where he'd find him.

15

The village they called Agnes sported a church steeple. Slocum had seen it against the starlit sky when he and Willa came into town on foot not to give away they were there. In the predawn's cool air, the two of them met and squatted with his four men. Diego, who they felt the outlaws knew the least about, had gone the night before to scout the place.

"There were three of them inside the Los Olevos cantina," Diego reported. "They had a big fiesta here last night. I saw Silva—he was here then. And he had some different men with him. Some of them might be passed out in the hay shed."

"You did good," Slocum said. They located the snoring pair. One was lying with a naked woman they awoke and who Willa quickly quieted with a hand over her mouth while they bound and gagged the two men.

"Chako and his cousin Alito," Trevino said under his breath. "They are a gang member too sometimes. That leaves Ortega, Carlos, and Silva if he is here."

143

"Carlos has red hair," Trevino continued. "And Ortega will sure kill you if you give him a chance."

"We're not going to let him do that," Slocum said.

After binding and gagging the two they found in the barn, they started for the rear door of the cantina. Slocum held his team up from entering the back door—two women were working in the kitchen. He stepped in to the doorway with his finger to his mouth to silence them.

When he moved inside, their large dark eyes flew open and they dropped the knives they were using to cut up meat and vegetables with.

"Hush," Slocum said with a frown for them. "Nothing will happen to you if you're quiet."

The older one nodded. "*Sí, señor*, we will be very quiet." Then she guided the teenager over into the corner partially shielding her as the rest of his men walked inside.

"Good," Slocum said and nodded to his men. The six-gun cocked in his fist, he headed for the doorway that led into the barroom.

When he stepped in to the dimly lit room, he heard a chair scrape and he whirled. The movement of someone going for a gun was all he needed to shoot the man in the shadows. He staggered forward and spilled facedown, but the rest flushed like quail. Someone dove out the open window. Slocum shoved the man in his way aside and tried to get his gun arm and head out the opening to shoot at the escaping one. But his target rounded the corner and was out of sight before he could shoot after him.

"Trevino, Cordova, and Jimenez get out back and try to find him. I'm certain it was Silva that got away. Diego and I can handle these in here."

Trevino shoved a big man facedown on top of a table, and then he went out through the back way after Cordova with Jimenez on his heels. The three, brandishing pistols in their hands, left in a hurry. Diego held his Colt on the other two while Slocum disarmed them.

"You must be Carlos?" he said to the red-headed outlaw.

"Who are you?" The man held up his bloody wounded arm. "I need a doctor."

"No, you don't. You won't bleed to death before your lynching." Standing right in the outlaw's face, Slocum reached down, unbuckled the man's gun belt, and let it drop. "You better start making your confessions with God 'cause you ain't got long to breathe on this earth."

"It's against the law—capital punishment—"

"We ain't the law from Mexico City—" Slocum removed two bowie knives from Ortega's body and tossed them aside. Then he jerked open the man's gun belt buckle and let the holster rig fall. "You too, Ortega, make your peace with God. They get back with your boss, he'll hang with you."

"You will never catch him." Ortega made a face, curled his lip in disbelief and disgust.

Filled with anger, Slocum wadded Ortega's shirt in his fist and drew himself up close to the outlaw's face with the muzzle of his pistol hard in Ortega's whiskered cheek. "Listen, you murdering, raping son of bitch, you're fixing to get what you deserve in a few minutes with or without Silva. You hear me?"

Ortega never answered him when Slocum shoved him toward the rear. "Bring Carlos along, Diego."

"Yes, sir. Pick up these guns and knives," Diego told the trembling bartender. "And all of them. I'm coming back for them."

"*Sí, sí, señor.*"

Slocum smiled to himself at the young man's orders as he propelled Ortega through the kitchen, and once outside in the starlight, he saw his other men coming back empty-handed.

Trevino shook his head warily. "He must have stolen a horse."

"We have these two and the two tied up in the barn. Find their horses and we're going to solve their problems," Slocum said.

Willa marched her two out of the barn. They were all put on horses, bareback, on leads and taken out of the village to a place over a half mile from anyone's jacal. Nooses were made. Then the ropes were strung over limbs in the larger cottonwoods. The four men were blindfolded and each one had the noose set beside his left ear to snap his neck when he and the horse parted.

"Anyone want to speak their piece?"

"Shoot me," Carlos said in a coarse voice. "I do not want to die by hanging."

"Is it worse than hell for you?"

"Yes, much worse."

"Good."

"Aren't you going to shoot me?" he moaned.

"No. Get ready, boys, this party is about over."

Each of one of his men stood behind a horse to slap the horse with a coil of rope out from under the condemned at his signal.

"Now! And may God have mercy on your souls."

The horses exploded and the ropes went tight with a shrill creak. The four dangled with their necks broken. Except for an involuntary kick or two, they were dead and delivered. Slocum nodded to the others. A job well done.

"Where will Silva go next?" he asked.

"The border," Cordova said.

"We will get some supplies and ride there. There are not that many places to hide around here." Slocum nodded to Willa, who'd joined them when they left the hanging scene. She handed them reins to their horses and everyone mounted.

"We're going north." Slocum reined his horse in close.

She agreed with a sharp nod.

On the move, they ate jerky and washed it down with tepid canteen water. A woman on the road that Slocum talked to had seen a rider a few hours ahead of them, riding bareback, hatless and looking over his shoulder a lot.

He thanked her and paid her twenty centavos. She smiled at the coins in her palm and nodded her approval of him.

"God be with you," she said after him.

They reached a small village before sundown. A small livery agreed to feed their animals. They unsaddled them and the short man put feed bags on each animal's head.

"A hatless rider came through here earlier?" Slocum looked around to see any sign of Silva.

The livery man they called Paco nodded. "But he bought a sombrero and a fresh horse from me. He was a mean *bastardo* and I was afraid he might hurt someone, so I sold him a fresh horse too cheap and he left me a worn-out *caballo*."

"I understand. Any idea where he was going?"

"He asked me about the road to St. Claire."

Trevino nodded. "We know that place."

"I've been there once or twice," Slocum agreed, recalling the small village. "Did he sound familiar with the water sources on the way across that desert?"

Paco shook his head. "I think he thought he could find them without help."

Cordova stepped in, chewing on a straw. "He will find them maybe, maybe not. There are some long kilometers between water holes by the way he goes."

Slocum nodded, considering it. "But he will be at them before we are. We need to approach all of them with caution. He might poison them."

"How will we know?" Trevino asked.

"Everyone will go to the different stores and ask if anyone bought any poison and what he looked like. He had to buy it here because he left Agnes bareback and had nothing to carry it in."

"Do you think he would—" Willa shook her head in disgust. "Only a cruel man would poison people at public watering places."

"You answered that yourself," Slocum said, hugging her shoulder.

"I guess so."

Later, they rejoined at the livery. Willa had found a woman who was a vendor. The older woman set up to make them supper with her small stove, frijoles with goat meat and handmade flour tortillas big as blankets.

They were all squatted on their boot soles. Jimenez told them the old man at the small store said he sold a stranger some rat poison who he described as looking like Silva.

Slocum nodded. Willa delivered him a large burrito he had to hold in both hands and he thanked her. The tortilla was hot in his fingers, but he knew from the smell, the contents would flood his mouth with saliva. She went back to get more for the others. Everyone served, she came back and poured coffee in their cups. The old woman continued to work, and soon had several smaller tortilla rolls filled with spicy cooked apples on a tray for them.

Slocum nodded in approval. "You did good, girl."

"Where will we go?"

"Our horses grained and watered, we will head up in the desert to spend the night. I don't trust villages to sleep in unless that I know someone who lives there."

The others agreed with a nod.

"How far is the border?" she asked.

"Three to four days' ride," Cordova said.

Trevino nodded. "I never would have thought about poisoning something as essential as a water hole. But as you say, he is a madman and if he thinks we follow him he will do anything to stop us."

Slocum nodded.

With the sun gone, they rode on a few miles under the stars finding a wide place along a dry wash with some dry grass for the horses. They rode far enough up the bottom so someone wouldn't stumble over them at night.

Slocum shouldered his bedroll, rifle in his other hand, and he and Willa hiked up the draw until they were well beyond the others. He dropped the bedroll on the ground and she sat astraddle it undoing the leather ties. With the side of his boot, he cleared the rocks and twigs from a place where they'd sleep. That completed, she rolled it out. Seated on her butt, she fought off her right boot, then the left one in a flashy exposure of her shapely legs that made him smile admiring the show.

She rose facing him, and unbuttoned the blouse and put it on the brush. The white lacy top shone in the moonlight as she undid the skirt and topped the bush with it. Then the silky, white chemise came over her head and hung loose in her arm.

She halted seeing he wasn't moving to undress. "You need help?"

"No, just admiring the scenery."

She shook her head in disapproval and fought the undergarment completely off. "You're free to look, I guess."

"Good, I'm broke."

"Oh, do you need money?" she asked, stepping close and undoing his gun belt.

"Enjoy life," he whispered softly in her ear. A person's life was too damn short to squander. With women in his life like Willa, he felt fortunate enough to be alive and share these breath-stealing moments with someone as sexy as she was. He swept her up in his arms and kissed her. Her fleshy stiff breasts poked into him as she eased his gun belt to the ground. Then she threw her arms around his neck, standing on her toes to get all of his mouth-to-mouth tasting he could give her. The birth of her eagerness excited him and he squeezed one of the rock hard boobs turning to stone.

With trembling fingers, she tore open his pants. They fell to their knees and he felt her hands on the bare skin past his underwear, followed by the release of his already large probe and her small fingers quickly clenching it. Then she shoved the underwear off his shoulders and they stripped it down, with him rising to free himself of all of his clothing and the cooler night wind sweeping his bare skin.

She opened the bedroll and pulled him down on top of her. His throbbing erection aching for her, she raised her butt and spread her knees apart. In the starlight looking down at her, he could see her closed eyelids and the look of anticipation on her face as he began to enter her gates.

"Oh, my God, Slocum." Her fingernails dug in his arms as she held her breath with her back arched for his entry. "What will I ever do without you?"

He could feel the growing spasmodic contractions inside her tight shaft that began to muscularly grasp his skintight hard-on, and he began to punch her deeper and deeper.

Her breathing grew swifter and his efforts harder and harder, until they were lost in a giant whirlpool that sucked them into a fiery tornado. And he came in a hard forced explosion. They collapsed in a pile.

He kissed her hard and she swept the hair from her face with the back of her hand. "Good God. That was the best yet."

He nodded, lying on his side facing her and softly fondling her breast. "Could have been, but they've all been nice."

"I won't call them nice." She rolled over on her back and looked at the stars. "I would call them wonderful."

"You know that when you are safe at the border, I'll have to ride on."

"Why?"

"Oh, there's those Kansas deputies on my back trail. It's time they caught up with me. Crook or his staff wouldn't tell them a damn thing, nor would the officers over at the fort, but some drunk soldier in a bar will let it slip as I told you before. 'Why him? Hell, he's off in Mexico scouting them 'Paces.'"

"Can they arrest you in Mexico?"

"Naw, but they can pounce on me at the border."

"Why don't you stay in Mexico?" She rolled over on her stomach and braced herself up on her elbows.

"I guess I get tired of the language and yearn to hear English spoken in a drawl."

"Hellfire, can't you get a pardon?"

"No, that old man owns that judge and jury in Kansas."

"I see."

He spanked her muscle-hard ass and laughed. "You won't be easy to forget."

"Good." With that said, she scooted over against him and reached for his dick. "I don't want to miss any minutes I have left with you."

Oh, my. Here we go again.

16

Mid-morning, Trevino rode back from scouting ahead, shaking his head. "There are two dead wild horses at the next watering hole."

"That no-good son of a bitch," Slocum swore. "You think it's been poisoned?"

"Yes, there's also several dead birds around it too."

"Better them than us. Cordova? How far is the next water?"

"Maybe we should go west to the village of Aqular. It is not on the way, but they have good water there."

Slocum looked over his crew for an answer. "How much further is dependable water if we keep on toward the border?"

"Maybe thirty-forty miles." Cordova grasped the great wooden horn on his saddle and rocked back and forth with a grim set to his face.

The vast azure sky covered a lot of country growing cactus and bitter greasewood with purple saw-edged mountains standing far off to all sides. Any edge they'd have over Silva gathering some hired guns would be lost if they didn't arrive up there soon after he did. Such a detour for them might give him one or two days to employ more gunslicks. Time enough to prepare for their arrival. Still, to chance losing horses or anyone in his party was too great of a risk—they'd better ride to Aqular.

"We best go find that village. Silva can wait," Slocum said.

The men around him on the circle of horses nodded, looking relieved. He never doubted for a minute they wouldn't go either way—but if Silva could poison one water hole, he could poison the next one as well.

With the blazing orange sunset dying in the west, they reached the small hamlet in a grove of cottonwoods. At the village's well, they dropped heavily out of the saddle. The horses dropped their muzzles in the water tank and slurped up gallons of water. Diego began working the pitcher pump handle to try and keep up with man and beast.

Willa, who had left them, returned with a vendor who had many things she offered to fix for them. Everyone squatted down around her with their thirst somewhat quenched and their sunbaked faces washed. The lady cooked and sang ballads while Jimenez played his mouth harp to accompany her. Some of the town women soon joined them, waving around bottles of red wine, and the liquid spirits began to flow. Soon his men were dancing in the dust with them. Seated on the edge of the tank, with Willa, watching them, Slocum nodded his approval.

"How quick these people can party," Willa said, hugging his arm.

"In this land you don't want to miss an opportunity."

"I understand. I understand."

He squeezed her shoulder—damn, she made good company.

The next morning, they took breakfast before dawn from the same woman and then rode north. Slocum felt their night's rest—though some had less than others—made his crew more alert-looking in the saddle. At least they were smiling. They still lacked two or more days to reach the border and then find their man.

"Someone is coming after us," Cordova said, looking back.

Frowns were exchanged at the sight of the dust and the effort the rider was making. Everyone reined up and waited. Obviously, whoever this person was, he wanted to join them.

"You boys make a husband mad?" Slocum asked, and they all laughed but Willa.

He gave her a slight shove and wink.

"Señor. Señor." The man reined in his lathered horse in a sliding stop. "My Captain Hernandez wishes for you to join him."

"What for?"

"He needs someone to steal the caisson from General Garcia."

"Huh?" Slocum frowned at the man. "Why us?"

The man looked around the desert like he was being sure no one could hear him. "If he steals it, Garcia might start a war. If you steal it, all he can do is cuss a gringo, no?"

"I'm not very wild about stealing that caisson. Besides, we're going after a murdering rapist named Silva."

"Ah, a bad hombre." He pulled his spent horse's head up. "My captain would pay you well for stealing it."

"How much?"

"Five hundred pesos a man, and her too."

Slocum cocked his eyes at the man. "Has he got that much money?"

"*Si, señor*. This is a very delicate thing."

"It is." Slocum hunched the gathered muscles in his shoulders. "This job might be damn dangerous too."

"Captain says you are the only man he knows in Mexico who could do this job."

"The only gringo dumb enough to try, he meant."

"No. No."

"Ride off over there." He gave a head toss for the non-uniformed sergeant to ride a short ways away. "Let me talk to my men about it."

"Oh, *sí*." He gathered his horse and rode apart from them.

Satisfied the man was far enough away, Slocum dismounted and pulled the crotch of his pants down. The rest climbed down too for him to explain the deal.

"That is lots of money," Trevino said. "I could live well on that much money for a year."

Slocum nodded. He understood the sum was high and represented a fortune to these men.

"We could all be killed," Jimenez said.

"Then we won't need the money." Cordova turned up his calloused palms. "It could be worse. We could have drank the water at that spring and died back there."

Trevino agreed with a nod. "I say we go steal that damn cannon."

"If you don't want to go with us, then I will understand. It's dangerous business, but the rewards won't be bad."

Jimenez rose to his feet, swept off his sombrero. "I want to go too."

Diego agreed.

"Willa?"

She looked hard at them around the circle, wet her lips, and then made a determined nod. "I want a part of this action. If anyone can steal that cannon, you all can do it."

Slocum waved in the sergeant and when he came close, he spoke to him. "I never caught your name."

"Sergeant Lopez."

"Sergeant Lopez, go tell your Captain Hernandez that we'll try to recover the cannon. Is it at Garcia's hacienda?"

"It is in the village nearby."

"What do we do with it when we get it?"

"Destroy it."

Slocum scowled at the man. Lopez obviously had no idea what a chore that could be. "That ain't easy either."

"That he can't use it, is all my captain asked for."

"I'll remember that," Slocum said, and the others nodded. So if they couldn't steal it, then destroying it would be just as good.

"I will tell my captain that you will handle it."

"Tell him we aim to try."

"Will you need anything?" Lopez asked.

"Yes. Three cases of blasting sticks, fuses and the caps to blow them up."

"Where do you want them?"

"You need to have them loaded on a packhorse outside of Ariba in two days."

Cordova gave a grim nod of agreement to Slocum's plan and added, "Have plenty of matches too."

"Ah, *sí*, I will have it all there."

Slocum watched Lopez ride off. All they had to do was steal a cannon from an army. Simple enough. "Let's ride."

The men put out their roll-your-own cigarettes under the heels of their boots and moccasins, then mounted.

"How far is this place?" Slocum asked.

"We can make it there in a day and a half. We'll be much closer to the border there too."

"I don't want to ride into that village—"

"Trevino has a cousin who lives near there," Cordova said.

"Can he put up all our horses and feed us?" Slocum turned in the saddle to look at the older man. "You know it could be dangerous for him if Garcia found out."

Trevino scoffed at the notion. "For a few pesos, Chico will do anything."

The others laughed. Slocum shook his head. This job could cost him his life if the general found out he'd supported them.

17

Chico's *rancho* was headquartered under a squaw shade in a side canyon with some water. There was a hand-dug well, a scattering of chickens, several goats, and two sleepy horses—mustangs with coats the color of a coyote. Two wives, both young, and several small thumb-sucking children who looked at Slocum's small army in wonderment. Chico was a short man close to the half century mark in years. But obviously not past the age of reproduction.

Slocum and Trevino squatted in the sandy ground away from the ramada talking softly to the man about what they must do.

"If we pay you twenty pesos for feeding us and our horses will that be enough?" Slocum asked.

The old man, whose wrinkled face looked like oak leather, nodded. "That would be most generous of you, Señor."

"You know, if Garcia ever learns that we were here, he might seek revenge on you and your family."

"He is a bastard. But I don't fear him."

"I'm sending Diego into the village tonight to find out what we need to be prepared for in there."

"I hope you take all of his gold." Chico laughed aloud and slapped his legs.

"We will see." Slocum wanted no mention to anyone of their true intentions—let him think it was the general's gold they were after. Besides, who would dare steal a cannon from this pompous general? Why, the whole situation was too ridiculous to even consider. At times he even thought so too.

Diego left under the shield of darkness to sneak into the village. Before he left, Trevino warned him that if the general caught him, he'd be forced into military duty and to be careful. The young man promised to watch out, and Chico told him that his youngest wife Lawanda's sister Juanita worked in the Rosa Cantina. She would conceal him if he told her Chico Noreaga sent him.

Hours after the youth left, Slocum stood under the star-pricked sky wondering about the boy's success. They couldn't dare stay long this close to the village or near the hacienda—word of strangers escaped fast back to men like Garcia who paid well for such information.

"When will Diego be back?" Willa stood close by.

"Whenever he's found the location or knows it is impossible for us to try."

"Is that word in your vocabulary?"

"Which one?"

"Impossible."

"Yes." He took and hugged her head to his body. "I use that word."

"Not very often."

He turned his ear to listen. "He may be coming back."

"So soon?"

"No one else would ride that hard up this canyon at night."

She snuggled her face and body up against him. Then they hurried on under the stars down to the ramada. The others were already there.

Diego leaped off his horse and gulped for breath coming up the sandy bank. "I found it. It is parked in a livery stable as he said. The guards are drunk and were passed out when I found it. There are some fancy horses and harness in those stables too."

"Did you see Lopez and his blasting powder?"

"No sign of him."

"Damn," Slocum swore. "Sounds like tonight is the night to take it. Get your horses, maybe he will show up."

"What if he doesn't?" she asked.

Slocum shook his head. For the moment, he had no good answer. "Then we can wreck it somehow so he can't use it."

In minutes. their horses were saddled and he paid Chico, who told them to come back. They headed across the moonlit desert in a hard drive. At the edge of town, they dismounted and Willa gathered their reins. Diego in the lead, they went on foot by the back alleys and dark side streets, crossing apart from each other through the sections lighted by cantinas and walking slow in case they were noticed.

At last they were in the livery. Quickly they bound and gagged the unconscious guards. Diego remained the lookout at the front door while they harnessed the three teams of horses.

"You and I can ride them," Slocum said to Cordova as they hitched the impatient ones to the caisson.

"*Sí.* It looks like fun."

"I've done it. They steer good." Slocum straightened from hitching a singletree.

"How do you figure they got this gun?"

"It was stolen somewhere from the U.S. Army. I can see the marks and insignias on it. This was never sold to anyone."

"Should we take it back?" Cordova asked with a grin that made his teeth shine even in the half-light.

"How far is the border?"

"Where we can cross? Oh, forty miles."

"Hell, yes, let's try."

"Someone is coming," Jimenez whispered.

"Don't shoot." It was Lopez. "I have the blasting powder. I didn't think you would get here so soon."

"Get it in here. Start arming sticks of it and tie two of them together." Slocum waved him to go after them.

"My horses are down the street," Lopez said.

"Go. Go."

"Should we wait for him?" Trevino asked.

"Yes," Slocum said. "We can turn back any pursuit throwing dynamite at them or setting it off in their path."

The older man agreed. "Besides, we have several hours till daylight."

Out of breath, Lopez ducked his head to ride his horse and the pack horse on the lead inside the stable's open front doors. Caisson teams hitched, they began to arm the blasting sticks. The older ones showed the younger ones.

Soon they had sacks filled with armed ammunition. One hung on Lopez's saddle horn and Cordova issued him two large boxes of matches. Trevino, Jimenez, with Diego all bore a sack on their back with boxes of matches to go join Willa and their horses a few blocks away.

Slocum gave them some time before he and Cordova each rode opposite horses out of the livery and down the street in a jog, with the three teams hauling the cannon behind. Late as it was in the night, few people acted interested. Drunks waved at them, and they soon were beyond all the jacales and barking dogs.

"Where are we taking it?" Willa rode in close to him, looking over the operation as they went along.

"To the border."

"Can we make it there?"

"Hell, yes."

She shook her head in disbelief. "You're a wild man, Slocum."

"Maybe that's why you like me."

"What if he sends an army after us?"

Slocum winked and nodded at Cordova. "We may have to stop and use the cannon on them."

Willa shook her head at him, spurring her horse in closer to him. "How much ammo do you have?"

"Three or four rounds, I'd say, in the box back there."

"When will he find out about his loss of the gun?"

"Not for hours, I hope. Tell Trevino I want him to fall back when it gets light and use my glasses. He can tell if and when they're coming."

"Can you really use this cannon?" She shook her head as if still in disbelief.

"Yes." He'd shot such weapons hundreds of times in the war. How accurate he'd be with this one he wasn't certain, but he could use it, and any shot near the pursuers would be sufficient to change their hearts about chasing them, but they'd save it for last.

"Cordova, come dawn you'll be the driver and one of the boys can ride in your place. I'll set the charges."

"*Sí*, this is much fun. To steal a gun like this so easy is beyond my dreams, hombre."

"Don't count chickens too soon, they ain't hatched yet."

"Eeha!" his man shouted, and they hurried off in the night.

Dawn, and they were less than four hours from the border by Cordova's calculations. Slocum's belly had begun to complain. There was some old adage about a soldier with an empty belly fought twice as hard as a well-fed one. In another half hour, there would be light leaking over the eastern crown of the small saw-edged mountains.

Lopez dropped back and rode beside Slocum. "Do you plan to give this gun back to the army?"

"Someone stole it from them."

"You think Garcia did that?" Lopez asked over the sounds of the caisson rims rolling along and the harness chains jangling over the hoofbeats.

"No, I think he bought it from a thief."

"I do too. My captain has wondered since you told him about it. He even had spies go see if it was for real. There is word Garcia had hired a gringo to come down there and show his men how to fire it."

"Had he come?"

Lopez shook his head. "Not yet that I know about."

"Good. This gun is of no use unless you know how to charge and fire it."

Lopez agreed and turned off his horse.

Diego soon reined his horse around and came in close to the teams and the rolling caisson. "Señor, there is dust back there. I think they are coming."

Slocum nodded that he heard the young man. "Tell Willa to bring my horse. You can ride with Cordova."

"Ah, *sí, señor*. I would like that."

Slocum nodded, and the boy rode off to catch her, leading the extra horses at the head of the line.

"Are there solders at the big spring?" Cordova shouted.

"Yes, black ones from Fort Huachuca. They'll damn sure fight if Garcia wants one."

Cordova looked back and then shook his head. "It'll be close."

"Ah, we'll get there." Slocum saw her coming back and reined in the teams. The hard-breathing animals were ready for a break.

Diego rushed in and dismounted. He pulled two boxes of matches out of his shirt and handed them over. Slocum took them and then boosted the boy up. He quickly transferred the sack of explosives from Diego's horse to his own.

"Cordova, short of the border, wheel that cannon around, unhitch it, and I'll be there to load and fire it. If Garcia won't quit before he gets there he will under cannon fire."

His man nodded that he understood, and they were off again. Willa smiled at him, her face under a veil of dust. Then she hurried to the front of the line with her wards.

Trevino joined him. "Where will we set the first explosives?"

"In that sandy wash about ten feet apart."

"That will be easy enough."

"That's why I chose it. We can plant them easy in the sand."

They rode over, and the charges were all set in the path of the Garcia's men. They'd be forced to come off the high bank at this break in the wall. The men coming couldn't avoid it. But the timing of the charges worried Slocum. His experience with these detonating cords' burning time was nil.

He and Trevino set them, and then he sent his man up on the rise to see how close they were. Slocum could hear the drum of their hooves. Soon, the older man and his horse bailed off the top and he shouted, "They're coming."

Slocum set the fuses, mounted his horse, and they both fled the wash.

The shouts of the men when they reached the tall brink of the wash was loud and then the explosion went off. A great plume of dust billowed high in the sky. Horses screamed and men cursed. Slocum nodded. He and Trevino fled on their mounts across the desert to catch his crew, who were a small speck north of them.

Short of the tall familiar cottonwoods of the Bernallio Springs that surrounded the small lake on the American side, his cannon was set up ready for him to load.

Slocum slid his horse to a stop and looked back. There were still riders coming, but not nearly as many. He winked at Cordova. "Get that ram."

The tied-on ram's end was covered with sheep wool. Slocum lugged the powder charge to the muzzle and slipped it in the barrel. "Now easy, tamp it down."

He went back for a cannonball. Actually an explosive grenade in that form. The company of black soldiers were armed and all lined up on the American side to watch the show. Slocum could hear them making bets on how close he could get to them.

"Will this hit them?" Cordova asked, tamping in the ball.

"I'm not certain." He fused and lit it. The cannon bucked and discharged its load. The shot whined through the air, fell to the right of the on-coming riders, and exploded, but the explosion spooked their horses wildly sideways and jarred men out of their saddles.

"Here," a white officer said, and strode over the unmarked line of the border. "I can sight that weapon."

"Good," Slocum said. "That all right, Sergeant Lopez?"

"*Sí, señor*. They aren't getting this gun back. That's my job."

They reloaded and the officer made adjustments. He straightened and nodded to Slocum, who set off the fuse. The cannonball went screaming out through the air, and must have landed to explode in the center or close to the area of Garcia's still-hard-riding men. The buffalo soldiers cheered. When the dust cleared, it was obvious that Garcia's army had given up.

"My name's Josh Silverton," the officer offered him a handshake.

"I was sure glad to see you. Thanks," Slocum said. "You've had more experience than I did with a cannon. Now, since it was stolen from some army outpost, it is yours to take back to the fort."

His arms folded over his chest, Silverton shook his head. "How in the hell did you ever get it back?"

"By raw nerve, I guess. Captain, allow me to introduce Mrs. Malloy."

The six-foot-tall officer with a hint of gray at the temples swept off his hat in a most gentlemanly way. "I've heard about you too, ma'am. You have the freight contract for the fort, right?"

"Yes, you must be new there?"

"I am, four weeks is all, Mrs.—"

"My name is Willa."

"Yes, ma'am."

Slocum wanted to laugh. The captain looked absolutely enthralled by her even under two coats of road dust. Wait till he saw her cleaned up.

"I don't think Garcia wants that gun back. Meet Sergeant Lopez of the *federales*. These others too."

Slocum and Willa shared a private nod. Silverton bore the appearance of a sharp officer. Doing his duty with a company of buffalo soldiers protecting the springs from any renegade Apaches getting a drink moving from Mexico to Arizona or vice versa. Bernallio Springs had been a way station especially for the Chiricahuas for a long time in their migrations from the Sierra Madres to the Dragoons. The buffalo soldiers prevented that traffic.

"I think Garcia went back," Trevino said.

"I would too," Slocum agreed.

"Where do we go next?" Trevino quietly asked Slocum as Silverton stood aside from them and talked to Willa.

"I want Silva." Slocum watched the black soldiers admiring the caisson at last back on U.S. soil.

"Where do you reckon he went to in Arizona?"

"Somewhere over near Bisbee. I think he might be at Tombstone looking for some toughs to join him."

"How will we find him?"

"Split up and we'll meet at Fort Huachuca in five days. They will let me stay there. I'll check out Tombstone and that area along the San Pedro River. Get any word let me know. I can accept telegrams at the fort too."

"We will need some money," Trevino said.

"I have some. Should be enough. Lopez can send me our money and I'll get it to you."

"Sí, señor. I will get my captain to send it to you at the fort."

"No. You can bring it to me at the fort," Slocum said.

"I will do that. No one else could have stolen that caisson from Garcia like you and these men did."

"We got lucky," Slocum said. "Damn lucky, but these are good men who ride with me."

Lopez agreed.

They parted with Silverton.

18

Tombstone's palaces of sin, liquor, and around-the-clock gambling roared twenty-four hours. Piano keys tingled; raging drunken whores paraded equally inebriated customers down the boardwalks to their cribs. A few men passed out or sat in a drunken state on the porches. Some leg and arm amputees in threadbare army uniforms, both blue and gray, begged on the corners.

Shysters on every cross street were selling worthless watches and other jewelry as valuable as the timepieces. Businessmen in aprons swept off the boardwalk in front of their businesses and ran off any old alcoholic residing there with the same broom.

Dusty, hipshot horses were at the hitch racks out in front. People passed by on bicycles, in buggies, and others in weathered gray wagons A beer hauling rig was parked at the Palace and in his long-tail, black coat and flat-crowned hat, Marshal Virgil Earp stood against the wall in front of the saloon and hotel.

"Well, Slocum, what brings you to this hellhole?" Virgil

said, giving his mustache a twist. "It has to be either money or pussy."

"I'm looking for a man who's called Leon Silva in Mexico."

"No telling what name he'd use here."

"That's what I said—in Mexico."

"Go behind this street"—Virgil motioned some toward the south—"and try that row of cantinas. Them Messicans may know about him."

"Who do you trust down there?" Slocum narrowed his vision against the glare off the street to study a shapely-looking woman coming out of woman's dress store. Natalee— Natalee Farley. What was she doing in Tombstone? Interesting enough.

"Adriano, the bartender in the La Paloma. He keeps secrets for a fee."

"Good, how's the law doing?"

Virgil smiled. "In this hellhole it never goes well."

"I'll see you."

"Keep your head down." The lawman smiled again.

"I will."

Slocum found the La Paloma cantina, and was forced to duck coming in the batwing doors or hit his head. Constructed from twisted mesquite posts, slab lumber, and covered in rusty sheet iron, there was nothing about prosperity in the place. The bar, set on beer kegs, had been sanded smooth and showed the scars of fights and idle sculptures. Artwork on the back-bar wall showed various paintings of naked women and couples having sex. The males were all well endowed, with long scrotums that hung to their knees, which would have made a billy goat proud.

Adriano was polishing glasses and alone in the mid-morning calm.

"They tell me you know everyone in Tombstone with a Mexican name." Slocum put three silver pesos on the bar.

"Oh, Señor, I know many of them." The handsome man smiled as if embarrassed.

"Marshal Earp says you can keep a secret too."

"*Sí.*"

"Is Leon Silva in town?"

"He was here yesterday."

"Where is he staying?"

Adriano looked around. "I think on the Santa Cruz over near Tubac."

"You know of a name over there?"

"Francis, his brother, farms over there I think."

Slocum dug out two more cartwheels and thanked him. "*Gracias.*"

He ducked his head going out the doors. On the porch, he let his eyes adjust to the glaring sun beyond the roof's edge. Searching around, he decided all the Hispanics were at work. On his horse, he headed back for the fort. Tubac was a hundred miles away. But it made sense for Silva to go there, where there would be more employable men in that valley than the silver mines who hired them all, including the Chinese.

His horse put up, he arrived after dark at the fort's visitors' residence under the rustling cottonwoods. The creak of the swing told him Willa was still up.

"You have any supper?" she asked when he mounted the porch steps.

"Some jerky."

"Learn much today?"

"Yes. He's probably at Tubac." He bent over and kissed her.

"Why there?"

"He has a brother named Francis who farms there."

"Lopez is in town. I told him you'd find him in the morning. He has the money. Your crew is there too."

"Good, I'll settle with them."

"They aren't going with you to Tubac?"

"I can't pay them much."

"I think they expect you to ask them to go along."

"I don't know." He herded her inside. "No guests tonight."

"No. But Captain Silverton is bringing in the caisson tomorrow. I think General Crook is coming down from Fort Bowie for the occasion.

"That will be a real newspaper story. Stolen caisson returned from Mexico and presented to the army. You ever hear where they stole it from?"

"No one is saying. The joke is the gun was never reported missing, the commander was so mad or embarrassed that he'd lost it."

"Oh, it is court-martial time."

She stopped at the door to the room and stood with her back against the wall. "I also learned those two deputies from Kansas were at Fort Bowie again. What do you say? A little whiskey, huh?"

"I figured they'd be here in time."

She fingered his vest. "I know tonight may be our last night. I don't want to talk about you going away. I want this to be the dream night of my life—understand?"

He closed his eyes and tried to recall a tougher parting. He took her in his arms and crushed her to him—words wouldn't work for him either.

19

They sat around the smoky campfire up in White Horse Canyon. Trevino, Cordova, Jimenez, and Diego all whittling. Sergeant Lopez squatted near them. Willa and Slocum sat on a log across from them.

A good-size shoat was on a spit cooking under her guidance and turned every little while. Slocum, Willa, and the men all were five hundred pesos richer, and discussed the trip ahead to Santa Cruz to search for Silva.

"My captain says if any one of you ever need a favor, he will try to repay you."

"Diego, ask him about your brother, Bigota," Cordova said.

"What is that?" Lopez blinked at them.

"My brother Bigota is in prison in Quaymas for a crime he never did."

"What is the crime?"

"They say he robbed a man, but he never robbed no one. The man who was to be his witness and tell the judge he wasn't even near the robbery was afraid they might make him guilty too."

"Bigota." Lopez nodded. "I see."

"It would be wonderful if he could come home."

"I will see what my captain can do for him."

"Willa's going back to her freighting business." Slocum looked up at them. "She said she would make jobs for any of you who want to work for her."

No one spoke up.

"We can ride over there in two days, locate Silva, and finish our business. I hope," he said.

"The pig will be cooked in an hour," she announced, and handed out bottles of wine.

So the final night was over late. Slocum told them a day of rest, and then those who wanted could ride with him over there.

On the appointed morning. they met at the local livery in town in the early hours before dawn. His four men and Willa all were there. They left in a long jog for the flat valley north of the Whetstones headed west.

By nightfall, they camped halfway to their goal at a small rancher's place. His gray headed wife, Ruby, fed them supper with Willa's help. Both she and her husband, Howard, acted overjoyed for the company. The adobe house was neat and snug underneath some twelve-foot-tall cottonwoods they'd obviously planted. They ate under a palm-frond squaw shade that she called house number one.

"Apaches ever bother you over here?" Willa asked Ruby over supper.

"Not bad. They stole our horses once. But we found more."

Howard agreed with a nod. "I simply guess we wasn't worth bothering with, huh?"

Everyone laughed.

Willa later told Slocum—Ruby and Howard were fearless people. Lying on his back studying the stars with her beside him, he agreed. "They're like a flower that grows up and blooms in the middle of the lane. Tracks on both sides—none in the center."

Tubac once served as a Spanish military outpost to protect the ranchers and farmers along the Santa Cruz River as well as the miners in the mountains around there. By this time, it was made up of a few stores, two cantinas, and a chapel.

Slocum sent Cordova and Diego into town to act like they needed work. The rest stayed in camp well out of town along the river.

After dark, the two returned to the place where they'd set up.

"Francis Silva is a large farmer downstream a few miles from here. Leon likes to frequent the cantinas at night, they say, and raise hell."

"When is he supposed to do that again?"

"Tonight." Cordova grinned big. "They say he lets everyone get drunk, then he comes. The bartender told us it is like he trusts no one."

"Hell," Willa said. "After the way you cleaned up his gang, would you blame him?"

They all smiled at her comments and shook their heads.

Slocum nodded. "We better saddle up. He's slippery. He uses hostages for shields. This is no simple-minded outlaw. The man has something that warns him or he's naturally cagy."

They waited in the alley until someone saw a rider come into the village and hitch his horse at the rack before Jose's Cantina. He looked around in the night like a mountain lion checking his territory before he went inside the rollicking bar. Music flowed. The *putas* shouted and danced. They didn't give a damn. The noise trailed out into the dirt street.

"That was him," Cordova whispered. Trevino agreed it was the killer from the mountains.

"Trevino, you and Jimenez cover the back door. Be sure before you shoot that it ain't us. Diego, you watch the front door in case he gets around us. Don't risk shooting an innocent bystander."

"I savvy."

With a head toss from Slocum, Willa took the horses back. He turned to Cordova. "When we go through that door, all hell will break loose."

Cordova agreed, both men rechecked the loads in their pistols and Slocum gave him a nod that he'd go in first. His shoulder swept the swinging doors aside. And the Colt in his fist belched fire and smoke. The lights went out and all the whores screamed. Someone tore out for the back door and Slocum shouted at Cordova, "He's going out the back way."

Moments later, Slocum stood in the back door and watched Jimenez sitting on the prostrate Silva and tying the reata around his ankle.

"We have that son of bitch right where we wanted him." Cordova ran for a horse and returned with Silva's. He took the rope from Trevino and set spurs to his mount. Silva was cursing loudly when Cordova went around the corner dragging him, but his cries soon changed to pain-filled screams when Silva, in a fast roll, was slammed into an adobe wall.

"Come on," Willa said, bringing them their horses on the run. "Cordova's headed for the river and a tree to hang him in."

Slocum looked around for Diego and he joined them. To keep the rest inside, Slocum unloaded his pistol in the air, then spurred his horse after the others.

On the ground groaning in pain, Silva moaned, swore, and cried. The silhouette of the cottonwood trees against the sky was over him, and the rustling of their coin-sized leaves on the night wind was orchestrated with the flow of the shallow Santa Cruz. A rope was soon slung over a large branch with a noose on the end dangling down.

They jerked Silva up and then set him on the horse that Diego held. Cordova stood on his own saddle and set the noose in place. Then he dropped down in the seat and said. "Good-bye, Silva, you son of a bitch. All this was for my little sister Leona, who you raped and gave her the clap, so she died in shame. May you pay in hell for that."

He took the coiled reata from his saddle horn, raised it high, and sent Silva's mount flying away. The outlaw's neck snapped like a shot and he was riding to hell on a fast horse.

Slocum shook their hands, thanking them. They all clapped him on the shoulder and told him they were proud to have ridden with him.

"Maybe we shall meet again, my amigos."

"Yes," they said in a chorus, and waved good-bye as he and Willa rode north.

"We get to Tucson tomorrow, I'm buying you a new outfit to wear," she said, riding beside him. "I ain't sending you off looking scruffy. Where are you headed?"

"Preskitt. It'll be cool up there. Then I may go to Colorado."

"Drop me a line."

"I ain't much on writing, but I'll try."

"For a guy I met in an army barracks one lonely night, you ain't much of a talker either."

"Willa. Willa. You'll find yourself a good man. Life's too short to pine over anyone forever."

"I'll try, big man. I'll try."

20

The *Tucson Herald* headlines read, "Famed renegade Chiri-cuhua Chief Whey reported dead in northern Sonora, Mex-ico. Reliable sources say ten days ago, the one known as Whey either fell off his horse in a swift river or had a heart attack and did the same thing. Authorities said Whey and members of his war party had been consuming copious amounts of stolen liquor at the time of his death. The whis-key was taken in a recent raid upon a pack train. . . ."

"What do you think of the story?" Willa asked, bringing his coffee out to him on the patio behind her Tucson house in the early morning.

Slocum dropped the paper and smiled at her. "I'd bet Nan Tan Lupan drinks some whiskey to that news."

"Let me read this to you. 'Santa Cruz Valley farmer Fran-cis Silva is offering a thousand-dollar reward for the arrest and conviction of the parties responsible for his brother Leon Silva's lynching last Tuesday along the Santa Cruz river near Tubac.

"'Local witnesses say a large mob came to the cantina in

Tubac, subdued Leon Silva, dragged him outside and down to the river location, where he was hung. Pima County Sheriff Hank Scott says that he has no leads on the parties responsible at this time, but will continue to investigate. Anyone with information should contact his office.

" 'According to his brother, Leon was a businessman from Mexico, in Arizona on a vacation.' " He put down the paper and smiled at her.

"Well, that cleans up a lot of things." She pushed her skirt underneath her to sit down on a chair opposite him. "And the stage for Preskitt leaves tonight at eleven. Here's your passes. I guess you know you change coaches at Papago Wells."

"Yes, I've rode it before." He reached over the table and captured her hands. "I have a new set of clothes. You even buy my way out of here. How can I repay you?"

"Stay."

"Oh, besides that."

"Maybe this afternoon, we can work that out." She gave him a sly smile.

"Your freighting business is doing well?" He released her hands and sat back in the chair to appraise her.

"Oh, yes. I'll get more involved in that now that you are going away."

He folded up the newspaper and put it on the table. "Well, I must say again. It's been a helluva time having you with me."

"A real helluva a time." she said and then shook her head as if she couldn't believe it had happened.

Slocum waited in the darkness across the street until the last minute to kiss Willa good-bye, and then he rushed across the street to the coach. The driver grumbled something about leaving his ass there, but finally let him in. The first smell of cinnamon assailed his nose, when he took a front seat facing the rear beside a woman whose stiff dress rustled when he sat down beside her.

"Good evening, sir," the business-dressed man facing him said as the driver undid the brake and shouted at his horses. "My name's George Goodwin."

"Good evening—" He hesitated. He recognized his seat companion. *Natalee Farley*. The stage's jerk start tossed them around some. but they recovered.

"My name's Slocum."

"Nice to meet you, sir. I just had told Mrs. Conley that this was my first trip to Prescott. Oh, I know that you local people call it Preskitt."

"Mrs. Conley," Slocum said, and tipped his hat to her, then turned back to Goodwin. "You will find it an arduous journey, sir."

At the Pichaco Peak way station, he had his first chance to speak to her in private while they changed horses. "Why the Mrs. Conley business?"

"I knew you'd have to know. When you got on that stage so late, I thought my cover was gone." She made a displeased face at him in the light coming from the stage stop's open front door.

"Cover?"

"Well, obviously I am traveling under an assumed name, so I must have something to hide, and I do."

"What's that?"

She looked around. The driver was headed for the coach door. With her skirt hem in her hand, she said under her breath, "I'll tell you later."

He climbed up after her. This must be a cat-and-mouse game. Where the pussy played with her victim and let him live a while longer, not knowing what she was going to do with him. And he was for damn sure in the dark as deep as the night that swallowed the small peaks around the location.

He'd met—actually found Natalee a few years before,

unconscious out in the middle of the Kansas prairie. The day of their meeting, her buckboard team had run off with her and wrecked the rig. He found the handsome young woman lying in the grass beside the upturned, splintered wagon. Not knowing where she belonged, he spread out his bedroll and made a shade for her. Since he knew of no doctor close by, he bathed her face with his kerchief and canteen water while he hoped someone'd show up to claim her.

A camp cook looking for her arrived after a few hours, wearing a food- and soot-stained apron, babbling about how was she doing.

"Fine. She'll be sore, but I think she's coming around."

Bleary-eyed, she sat up. "Hercules, are the cattle all right?"

He swiped off his beat-up felt hat and clamped it to his chest before he said a word. "Yes, Mrs. Farley, they're fine."

Braced with her hands on the ground behind her back, she blinked her baby-blue eyes at Slocum. "And I haven't met you, sir."

"Slocum, ma'am."

"I suppose you saved my life."

"No, but I figured you didn't need any more sun."

"Oh, Mr.—"

He cut her off. "My name is Slocum, no Mr. about it."

"You look like a drover," she said as if escaping her confusion and the aftereffects of the wreck. "I need a head man. Mine was shot three days ago."

"I'm on my way back from Abilene. I just finished delivering a herd up there for the Menenger Brothers."

"Oh, my." She held the back of her hand to her forehead as if having a spell. Then she sprawled on her back atop the bedroll, looking ready to faint again.

"You alright, Missy?" Hercules asked.

"I'll be fine, Hercules. You explain to your new boss what has happened to us."

Slocum, after talking over the herd's situation with Hercules, loaded the limp Mrs. Farley in his arms and carried her back to her cow camp. That afternoon he met with the crew and made certain everything was settled. She, in the meanwhile, recovered except for a bruise or two.

The next day, with things in hand in the camp, he rode into the Wichita Crossing to learn all he could about the shooting and find her a rig so she would have some transportation. He looked up a bartender the boys had mentioned called Cauldwell who worked in Coyote Slim's Saloon.

"A man named Zinc Ralston was shot in here two days ago?" Slocum asked the man who'd drawn him a beer.

"Right." Cauldwell held the glass he's been polishing up to the light. Satisfied, he stacked it.

"What was the story?"

"Some gambler named Joe Moore shot him over a card game. Ralston was drunk as all get-out and real mouthy that day. He couldn't have out drawn a gun fast enough against an eighty-year-old man. All at once he went to cussing at Moore, jumped up, and tried to draw his six gun. Far as I could tell, he simply got what he had coming."

Slocum thanked the man, paid for his beer, gave the him five silver dollars for his troubles and rode back to her outfit. He sent two of the boys in with the team and repaired harness to get her *new* buckboard.

Besides sipping lots of Natalee's honey each night out on the trail, the rest of the drive up to Abilene with her herd went smoothly. She paid him well for all of his troubles, after he got her top price for her cattle.

Now, seated beside her again on the swaying coach headed for Prescott, he considered some of those fine memories he had of her in bed with him. The sun was peeking up in the east when they made the next stopover.

The driver took a much longer layover in Casa Grand. Outside, Slocum caught her by the elbow and guided her to the side of the adobe building to find out the rest of her problems.

"I married—" She looked around the yard outside the stage stop to be certain they were alone. Then she turned her blue eyes back on him. "I married a man named—God, you sure look good."

Impulsively, she stood on her toes and kissed him. "Oh, Slocum, I'm in a terrible fix."

"How? Why? You tasted the same." Then he winked at her.

She blushed. "Damn you. I married this guy in Texas. Big mistake. He was under the impression that I would be the little woman and he would be the big man." A disgusted frown crossed her face. "That was my ranch. That was my money. None of it was his. Besides, I was not happy in the role of his little woman.

"So he went off to Mexico to buy cattle and he was going to send back for my money, he thought. I was all ready. As soon as he rode out of sight, I sold my ranch, drew all my money out of the bank, and left Texas. End of that story. Oh, I imagine he's on my back trail. What I need now is a divorce."

He pulled her up against his body and drew the cinnamon perfume up his nose. "Natalee, I bet we can have all of that arranged for you in Preskitt in no time at all and there won't be anything he can do about it."

"Oh, thank God, Slocum, you've saved my life twice now. How can I ever repay you?"

He hugged and rocked her ripe body hard against his own. "I can see now this job has got its rewards. Why, twenty-four hours from now we'll be in the Central Hotel—rocking the bed. How's that?"

"Oh, my God, I can hardly wait."

Neither could he. Neither could he.

Watch for

SLOCUM AND THE YELLOWBACK TRAIL

379th novel in the exciting SLOCUM series
from Jove

Coming in September!

DON'T MISS A YEAR OF

Slocum Giant
by
Jake Logan

Slocum Giant 2004:
Slocum in the Secret Service

Slocum Giant 2005:
Slocum and the Larcenous Lady

Slocum Giant 2006:
Slocum and the Hanging Horse

Slocum Giant 2007:
Slocum and the Celestial Bones

Slocum Giant 2008:
Slocum and the Town Killers

Slocum Giant 2009:
Slocum's Great Race

penguin.com/actionwesterns

M457AS0409

GIANT-SIZED ADVENTURE FROM AVENGING ANGEL LONGARM.

BY TABOR EVANS

2006 Giant Edition:

**LONGARM AND THE
OUTLAW EMPRESS**

2007 Giant Edition:

**LONGARM AND THE
GOLDEN EAGLE SHOOT-OUT**

2008 Giant Edition:

**LONGARM AND THE
VALLEY OF SKULLS**

2009 Giant Edition:

**LONGARM AND THE
LONE STAR TRACKDOWN**

penguin.com/actionwesterns

M456AS0409

GIANT ACTION! GIANT ADVENTURE!

THE GUNSMITH

J.R. ROBERTS

Little Sureshot And
The Wild West Show
(Gunsmith Giant #9)

Dead Weight
(Gunsmith Giant #10)

Red Mountain
(Gunsmith Giant #11)

The Knights of Misery
(Gunsmith Giant #12)

The Marshal from Paris
(Gunsmith Giant #13)

Lincoln's Revenge
(Gunsmith Giant #14)

penguin.com/actionwesterns

M455AS0509